HORRORific Tales

Volume Three

(Serial Killers)

Edited by Colin C. Martin

Serial Killers
HORRORific Tales Volume Three (Serial Killers)

Paperback Edition ISBN 978-1-0684637-2-3

Published by HORRORific Productions Ltd
61 Bridge Street, Kington, Herefordshire,
HR5 3DJ, England, United Kingdom

A CIP catalogue number for this title is available from the British Library

This book is dedicated to independent creators trying to make their way in the world. By honing your craft and not taking the easy payout from the bland, sterile corporations, you inspire us, spark our imagination and make us believe that anything is possible. Keep striving on your journey, stay true to yourself and may every success that you deserve arrive at your door.

Special thanks to Cameron, Chris, Del, Stephen and FL_3 for being my co-hosts, inner circle and close support as I've went on this creative journey. Here's to the beginning of something truly HORRORific!

Thank you also to the myriads of independent creators who have interacted with our podcast and publisher over the years. You have helped to inspire me to keep going and to put something out into the world.

The HORRORific Podcast is available on numerous platforms. Find us where you usually get your podcasts here:

They have practiced their craft. The rituals have been performed; the conditions have been set. Now they watch and wait for their intended. Who knows what tragedy, compulsions or simple evil drives these people to kill again and again. Once you are in their sights however, there is no reasoning, negotiation or escape!

Serial Killers

Contents

Introduction

Third time is a charm they say, and I do feel charmed to be able to bring you the next collection in the HORRORific Tales series. The response this time around has been amazing. Thank you to everyone that reached out with their stories. It's great to see word getting around about HORRORific Publishing.

Not only do we have returning authors who have taken part in previous volumes, but we have new writers coming on board as well. It's great to have this balance of regular and new voices for you to enjoy. We do everything we can to maintain a vibrancy to these collections.

If this is your first time picking up a collection of HORRORific Tales, then welcome. It's great to have you with us. Be sure to check out our other volumes in the series.

We try to do something a little differently here. Instead of presenting you with continual faceless names on a page you can get to know the creators behind the stories via The HORRORific Podcast. Many of our authors are regular guests on the show and we hold a celebration stream for each publication released.

Serial Killers

Our authors are horror fans just like you and enjoy talking about their love for the genre. Come on board during the live chats and say hello.

Serial Killers was a tricky one this time around. People love talking about them. These individuals bring out both a fascination and repulsion in our psyche. What drives them to do what they do? Are there times when their twisted logic makes sense? I honestly don't even think that they truly know the answers to these questions. One thing we can do as horror fans though is explore this phenomenon from the safety of these pages. Who knows? The person watching you right now might think that you are on to them!

I truly hope that you enjoy these stories. Everyone has pulled a blinder this time around in bringing unique and twisted tales to you. We have lots planned and are more than happy to have along as part of this journey.

Welcome to the HORRORific family and we look forward to seeing you again.

Yours in appreciation

Colin C. Martin

A PASSION SHARED

BY

GARY BATCHELOR

Friday 23rd December 2016

21:45pm

'So when did you leave Josh?'

Penny Styles looked from under her eyelashes at the cocky hunk before her.

'I kicked him out the middle of last month. He couldn't handle being overlooked for the manager's position and became apoplectic when he found out it was you who had got it.'

She reached out with her hand and laid it on one of his.

'He became so unstable that he began to do my head in and my work suffered. I think he was not only jealous of you, and what you had achieved, being ten years his junior, but my promotion and success weighed down on him as well.'

Simon Fortesque smiled broadly and covered her hand with his.

'Well, you don't have to concern yourself with Josh anymore, because I'm here to look after you.'

Penny raised an eyebrow, and a small frown crossed her face.

'But you're married Simon, with children. I couldn't possibly entertain any thought of starting an affair, no matter how attracted I am to you.'

She lowered her eyes again before looking up.

'I'll leave her and the kids. I want you Penny. You're smart and sassy and we'd make a great team.'

She allowed her eyes to roam over his fit carapace. He clearly worked out and took trouble over his appearance.

But is it too soon to jump into something so deep?

'Look Simon, I'm not going to say no at this point.'

Simon looked disappointed. 'I can feel a 'but' coming on.'

'It's too soon after Josh, I need a bit of space to clear my head. I hope you can understand that. Plus, if you're serious then you have to do something for me as well don't you?'

He brightened. 'Oh, I will, when I get home tomorrow.'

'But it's Christmas Eve, Simon. It's a bit heartless to tell your wife and children that daddy's leaving home to go and be with another woman.'

He considered a moment. 'Yes, you're right of course.'

He looked at Penny and a look of concern crossed his face.

'But what about you? I couldn't live with myself if I thought that you were going to be spending the festive season alone.'

‘Oh, I’ll be fine, don’t you worry. I’ve got plenty of friends and family, I won’t be alone at all I can assure you. Be glad to see the back of them before it’s all over I expect.’

She smiled to reassure him.

‘Well, I suppose we should mingle with the others shouldn’t we?’

Simon looked disappointed.

‘Yes, I suppose we, that is, I should. A manager must be seen to be networking and spreading his attention across the workforce.’

‘I’m so glad you accepted my invitation to the company Christmas Party.’

‘Well, I knew Josh wasn’t going to be here, so I thought ‘*why not*?’

‘Where is he by the way? Do you know?’

'Gone west I believe. Some final sales he had to make before the festive shut down. But that's not my concern anymore, is it?'

'No, it isn't. Well, I must circulate.'

Simon reluctantly moved away from her and began to infiltrate a group of four who stood a little away. Penny was relieved at the space. His intensity was getting a little overpowering.

That said, I haven't been completely honest with Simon.

When he had found out in early November, Josh had found it difficult to cope with being overlooked for the vacant manager post. His frustration had boiled over when it was revealed that Simon Fortesque had been the fortunate beneficiary.

'He's a lackey, a toady with no finesse or subtlety at all. He's all bish, bosh, bang,' he lamented.

My success and promotion at work had also played its part in bringing him down further. He never mentioned it, but I knew it was there.

But by far the biggest single factor in Josh's instability was the uncertainty he felt as the investigation into the rape and murder of the student, Rachelle Temple gathered momentum.

He knew he had been careless and risked not only his freedom, but mine as well.

Fortunately, Josh's reckless approach had, eventually proved to be inconsequential as the police moved on to other leads and suspects. That though had provided a warning that neither of us could afford to ignore.

But while he was in that fog of uncertainty, he began to unravel, and it became increasingly difficult for me to put the genie back in its bottle. And God knows I tried.

I returned to the here and now and found a man in his fifties standing next to me, offering to top up my champagne glass. I put my hand over the glass and politely declined.

'I'm driving so I'm only allowing myself the one,' I said.

'Ah a social conscience, very rare. You must be Penelope Styles, Josh's wife.'

'I am. And you are?'

'Yes sorry, forgive me. I'm forgetting my manners. I am George Venton, CEO of the UK subsidiary of Syntech Pharmaceutics.'

I appraised him carefully.

'Are you responsible for the recent manager position going to Simon Fortesque?'

'I was one of three on the interviewing panel, yes. I do hope that you are not going to create a scene Mrs Styles. Josh was very close to being appointed but in the end, there were just too many questions surrounding him. So, we chose Simon. Josh's chance will come, have no fear.'

She looked at him for a moment, remaining silent, seeing if he would fill it.

'I must say you look stunning in that outfit Mrs Styles. I do hope you can accept a genuine compliment.'

She smiled. 'I can, coming from such a distinguished looking gentleman Mr Venton.'

'Oh please, George.'

'Well George, I can assure you that I have no intention of creating a scene. These decisions are always difficult and there are always winners and losers. Josh is naturally disappointed, as indeed am I, but he remains committed to the company.'

'I'm so glad to hear that, Penelope.'

'Penny, please.'

A striking looking woman in her early forties came up to us and smiled warmly at me.

'Oh! Please may I introduce my wife, Rivka. This is Penny Styles, Josh's wife.'

Rivka held out a hand and I took it, briefly.

'I've met Josh a few times at these types of function. He is certainly a looker Mrs Styles.'

'And he has a brain as well. A PhD brain,' I stated proudly.

'Does he really? Well, George never revealed that.'

'Research wasn't for him though.'

Rivka glanced around.

'He's not here?'

'No. He's away. Some last-minute orders to sort for the New Year, I think. He has sent his apologies and festive regards to everyone.'

'Well, I'm sorry to drag my husband away but there is a phone call he must make, which I suspect in all the excitement, has slipped his mind.'

George smiled and mock played at being forgetful.

'Senility, you know.'

'I doubt that very much,' Penny said.

'Rivka is correct though. I must make a call. Do excuse me Penny. It's been a pleasure to meet you. I hope to have that pleasure again.'

'Oh, I think we can count on that,' I said.

They both moved away and as they did so from out of nowhere, Simon was by my side again.

'Chatting up the boss, good move,' he said, smiling.

'Your wife isn't here?'

Simon appeared irritated by my mentioning her.

'No, we couldn't get a babysitter, so she stayed at home.'

'Oh, that's a shame. It would have been so lovely to meet her.'

Simon looked at her as though trying to work out the meaning behind her words.

She remained silent, letting them echo around his head.

23:30pm

What do you mean you've got to go Jason?'

'I'm sorry but I did warn you Suzi. I've time for dinner and coffee after, but I have to leave before midnight. I've got to close a contract tomorrow, so everything is in place for the New Year.'

'But I spent a fortune getting a babysitter who could stay overnight, so that we could spend our first night together.'

'I'm sorry, I thought I'd explained all this.'

Suzi glared at him across the four-poster bed.

They had booked a room at the Hatherley Manor Hotel north of Gloucester just off the A38, after meeting up late afternoon, after he had concluded some business. They had booked in under assumed names and were therefore paying by cash.

Suzi walked around the bed and came up to him. He hadn't taken his suit jacket off yet and stroked his face.

'I'm sorry, am I rushing you?'

Jason smiled and reached out for her.

'No not really. But after my recent loss, I suppose I'm finding it difficult. Can you understand that?'

'Oh yes, all too clearly. I'll try and move a little slower. I don't want to frighten you off by leaping on you like a predator.'

She looked at him and slipped off his jacket so that it fell to the floor. She allowed her hands to track over the smooth tight shirt he wore marvelling at the taut, tense musculature beneath.

‘I enjoyed the gym session and swim. I’m so glad I let you persuade me to join you. Although I will admit to enjoying the health suite a little bit more.’

The health suite had consisted of a sauna, steam room and Jacuzzi and the pair of them had spent an hour frolicking and playing around.

‘I find it so easy to unwind in that environment. It was lovely to have you with me Suzi. It made such a change from being on my own.’

Suzi caressed his face again.

‘I understand if you miss your wife,’ she said. ‘It can’t be easy for you.’

‘I’m sure it isn’t straightforward for you either. I know you’ve told me about your husband’s repeated misdemeanours, but I don’t suppose it makes it any easier.’

'It doesn't. And in all honesty, I'm not proud of what I'm doing either. Two wrongs don't make a right as my mother used to say.'

Jason sat bolt upright.

'So, you're only here to get back at your husband?'

'No, I am not. I thought we'd been through all this before. I am unhappy with married life and I can see no way that my husband is ever going to change. He is a repeat offender, a recidivist where other women, girls are concerned. He can't help himself. There is nothing I can say or do that will change that. I could threaten him with divorce or losing the children or any other number of threatening scenarios and none of them would have any effect whatsoever.'

Jason appeared thoughtful.

'Does he not have a conscience? No empathy over what he is putting you through?'

'No none whatsoever.'

‘This surely can’t continue, can it? I mean haven’t you thought of any way out of this impasse, save you having affairs in retaliation? It’s not much of a life is it? How would he react to you having an extra marital relationship?’

Suzi smiled.

‘He wouldn’t give a shit. I have no value for him now. I’ve done my bit, bearing his children and supporting him. I mean, I live a very comfortable life, I want for nothing, but material possessions and money aren’t everything. There is so much more to life than conspicuous consumption.’

Jason smiled and nodded.

‘I’m with you on that one. Look, I do really have to go.’

Suzi cast her eyes down to the bed.

‘What line did you say you were in?’

'I'm with a well-known supermarket beginning with 'A', other outlets are available.

'Sales?'

'For my sins. So, what is your husband doing tonight?'

'Oh, it's the company Christmas who-can-I-find–to-fuck party.'

'And he doesn't take you?'

'Never. Not once.'

She glanced at the bedside clock. It was almost midnight.

'He's probably sussed his target for the night and is making his move on her right now. He's like a predator stalking his prey.'

'I really do have to go. Tell me. Does he always get what he wants?'

Jason stood and retrieved his jacket from the floor and put it on. He straightened himself out and made himself look presentable. Suzi lay back on the bed, inviting him to stay.

‘I think he probably does. He looks good and he has the gift of the gab. I suppose that’s mandatory in your line of work.’

Jason froze momentarily but recovered.

‘Our line of work?’

She looked up at him from beneath her eyelids and writhed on the bed as she began to undo the buttons on her silk blouse.

‘Sales.’

‘Oh yes, I see. Still, there must be the odd one or two who slip through his fingers.’

‘There could be. But there are always others who willingly take their place.’

‘You make it sound like a factory production line.’

‘That’s how he operates.’

Jason paused a moment.

‘Live by the sword, die by the sword,’ he said.

Suzi sat up looking at him.

‘Whatever do you mean by that?’

Jason smiled. ‘You did say he was like a predator stalking his prey, didn’t you?’

‘Yes, but I don’t quite follow.’

‘These things have a habit of catching up with the perpetrator, eventually.’

Jason could see the cogs turning behind Suzi’s eyes as she tried to fathom out what he was getting at.

Patience, patience.

00:25am

'It's been an absolute delight, my dear. Goodnight.'

George Venton shook Penny's hand warmly before Rivka intervened and took the same hand.

'A pleasure to make your acquaintance Penelope. Forgive our early departure, but my husband is not as young as he thinks he is and in any case, he has some business he must attend to.'

Penny smiled.

'Please, no apology is necessary. I quite understand the sacrifices that must be made to be competitive and successful.'

They were all stood out on the steps leading up to Markham House, the banqueting hall that had been used for the Christmas party. Penny watched as the chauffeur-driven Rolls Royce came around the drive and stopped at the foot of the steps.

The driver got out and opened the rear doors for George and Rivka. They waved at Penny as the car slipped effortlessly, noiselessly away.

‘Now the old fart has left maybe we can get this party started.’

Penny didn’t flinch or indicate in any way that she was caught by surprise. Without turning around, she continued to watch the Rolls as it glided down the drive towards the main road.

‘That isn’t a very pleasant thing to say about the man who has been responsible for your recent elevation in the company.’

Penny pirouetted and came face to face with Simon.

‘I’m the man responsible for my elevation in the company, no one else.’

Penny smiled humourlessly. ‘Of course you are. How could I not remember that. Shall we go back inside?’

Penny took a step forward, but Simon held onto her elbow, forestalling her.

'I thought we might leave ourselves. What do you say? There's a four star just five minutes away.'

Penny looked directly into Simon's eyes.

'I was thinking that it would perhaps be more fitting if we were to make our first night together tomorrow, Christmas Eve.'

A broad smile spread across his face and he encircled her waist with his arms.

'You took my breath away the moment I lay eyes on you. That gown is spectacular. It shows you off to maximum effect in such a subtle manner. It is exquisite. And so are you.'

He took her right hand in both of his and kissed it.

'Always such a gentleman Simon. It does you credit.'

She smiled warmly.

Simon looked at Penny with ill-concealed desire in his flaming eyes.

'I'll be an animal tomorrow night I can assure you.'

Penny's blue eyes twinkled. 'Oh, I think you can count on me being a bit of a beast too.'

Saturday 24th December 2016

21:45pm

Simon took a sip from his second Remi Martin and looked at Penny over the rim of the glass. He was finding it increasingly difficult to contain himself. Penny, for her part seemed to be control personified. It was beginning to gnaw at him.

'So did you tell me your wife's name?'

Simon grunted. They were back onto subject matter he had no interest in. Why did Penny insist on making all this small talk when there were desires to be sated?

‘Suzi,’ he replied in a monotone.

‘Have you always played around?’

What’s this? *Twenty questions*?

‘I’ve always had a roving eye in all honesty. But as the children came along, I suppose I began to find our relationship stale. She didn’t turn me on as much as she had in the past. She put on a bit of weight, began to let herself go I suppose. Not like you.’

‘But I’m probably ten years younger. I should look better, shouldn’t I? And I haven’t had any kids, so I’ve got an advantage there.’

'Well, I began straying more and more. It may have acted like a drug in the end. It helps your libido and your confidence if you know you can attract members of the opposite gender with amazing regularity. Haven't you ever wanted to try out another? Apart from me that is. Would you find that a turn on?'

Penny considered a moment.

'There was a young man once upon a time who caught my eye and who I think was attracted to me.'

'What happened?'

'Oh, I don't know. It just died a death really.'

Penny was referring to the first time she had killed. A student, twenty-year-old Cory Prior had come onto her. She had taken offence at his presumption. They never found his body.

'And that was it? The only occasion you've been tempted to stray away from Josh, apart from now. With me.'

'It would appear so.'

Penny reached for her glass of Rioja and took a sip.

They had finished the three-course dinner a little over twenty minutes earlier. Penny was well aware that Simon was getting impatient to get to bed, but she wasn't being herded into any provocative action until she was ready.

Simon finished his Remy Martin, draining the glass and laying it on the table with a flourish, as if to make a statement.

Penny smiled. 'Time for one more,' she said.

A brief frown swept across Simon's face before he tried to smile in acquiescence and indicated to a waiter that he would have another.

Penny smiled at achieving her goal so easily.

The drink duly arrived. Simon sipped it reverentially.

'I never drink to excess,' she stated.

Simon looked across at her.

'Do you think I do?'

'Oh no, I wasn't suggesting that at all. I was merely saying that I don't because, well, why would you want to dull your senses to other pleasures?'

'I quite concur. So, I won't be having anymore after I finish this one,' he said, raising his glass before taking a further sip.

'Do you want another Rioja?'

'No thank you.'

Simon seemed pleased that was the case.

'If you'll just excuse me, I have to go to the men's room.'

Simon stood up and made his way towards the toilets.

Penny watched his back disappear through the doorway and then counted to thirty before nonchalantly glancing around the room. There were few tables close to theirs that were occupied, so she felt secure in not being scrutinized.

She reached down and drew up a slim bag and opened it. She removed a small vial and placed it on the table, so it remained hidden from prying eyes. After giving the illusion of applying a little make up, she picked up the vial, removed the plastic stopper and tipped the powder into Simon's Cognac.

She replaced the sealed vial in her bag and lowered it to the floor. Her final act was to swirl the contents of the glass around so that the powder dissolved in the Cognac. She took a sniff of the contents and replaced the glass in its original place.

She glanced casually around the room as though she didn't have a care in the world. She was sure no one had witnessed what she had done.

Simon returned a minute later and resumed his seat. He picked up the glass and took a sip.

'Have you ever seen Josh with other women?'

Simon took a further sip before putting the glass down on the table.

'You know I don't think I have. Our paths have crossed no more than half a dozen times at the various company functions but he's always well behaved. Does have a habit of disappearing off on his own though, as I recall. We tend not to see him after he does that. Why do you ask? Are you having second thoughts about all this?'

'Oh god no. We are most definitely in the past. Time to turn the page. It wouldn't have surprised me if he did, that was all.'

'I would have thought you were enough for any man.'

Penny smiled and lowered her eyes.

'With that in mind, I wonder before we, retire, I would love to feel the wind blowing through my hair in your convertible. Would that be too much to ask?'

Simon rolled his eyes.

'Then I promise you I will show you everything a woman can do to please a man.'

'Of course.'

Simon drained the glass and stood. Penny stooped down and picked up her handbag.

They walked to reception where Simon asked for the car to be bought around the front.

'I'll just go to the toilet and freshen up,' said Penny and walked away.

Within four minutes the car was out front. Simon ambled down the steps and exchanged positions with the valet.

Unseen, Penny slipped out of the toilet and took the stairs to the room they have booked. She retrieved the small overnight bag that she had bought and made her way down the stairs.

She walked confidently to the reception desk, using the pillars as a blind so that Simon can't observe her from the car.

She exchanged a few words with the receptionist and then walked through the glass doors to the waiting Simon, who already has the roof down.

She held the small bag in such a way that it blended into herself and used her body to hide it as she reached the car door.

As Penny got in, she noticed that Simon wasn't looking too good. He smiled as she buckled her seat belt and forced himself to focus on her wish.

Simon pulled away and drove down the long drive, turning right onto the main road and roaring off through the gears.

'Where do you want to go?'

'Oh, not far darling. I'll let you know as we drive.'

After a few miles Penny could see, out of the corner of her eye that Simon was having difficulty concentrating.

‘Take the next left,’ she said.

Simon dutifully obeyed and they entered the Cotswold National Park.

She turned to him with yearning.

‘You know I think I want to fuck you outside. I know the exact place.’

Simon grinned and increased his speed.

They are driving along the B4068 towards Upper and Lower Slaughter, when they come to a crossroads.

‘Right here,’ said Penny.

Simon turned as they passed the edge of Upper Slaughter, continuing on this road until they arrived at a T junction with the A429, close to Bourton-on-the-Water.

'Right again.'

She glanced across at him, confirming to herself that he is becoming increasingly uncoordinated.

Simon turned onto the A429, and they travelled along this road before Penny turned to him.

'Veer off to the right onto the Old Gloucester Road, the A436 just ahead.'

Simon acquiesced although the turning took him some effort.

As they approached a crossroads Penny glanced at him again.

'Just stop at this crossroads darling and park up.'

Simon tried to break smoothly but instead brings the car to a juddering halt and it stalls.

He leaned towards her and smiled, leering at her as though he was drunk.

‘Better turn the ignition off.’

Simon complied.

He leaned towards her once again, but as he did so this time, she nimbly opened the car door and slipped out, surreptitiously clutching her bag.

‘Hey,’ he slurred.

She smiled and taunted him.

‘Catch me if you can.’

She disappeared into the darkness.

Simon sat in the seat increasingly bewildered by the turn of events. He is even more dumbfounded when a car engine started. Two dazzlingly bright headlights shine on him like a pair of spotlights and he closes his eyes at the glare, shielding his eyes with his hand. He heard the car pull away and watched, astonished, as it goes back the way that they he has just come.

'What the fuck,' he slurs.

He starts the engine, engages the gears, and with a four-point turn takes off in hot pursuit.

He can see the other car just ahead. As it reaches a junction it turns right. This will take them away from Lansdowne and towards three small villages, Hampnett, Northleach and Farmington.

As he pursued the car, Simon attempted to organise his muddled, confused thoughts into something more coherent. He is finding it increasingly difficult to stay awake and his body feels as though it is seizing up.

The A429 is a single lane carriageway but the car in front is cruising at over one hundred and twenty miles an hour. Simon put his foot to the floor to reduce the distance between them.

‘What the fuck is this bitch up to?’

He speaks aloud and his words are thick. He is finding it a struggle to maintain control of his muscles including around his mouth. He continued to mutter to himself but could find no answers to the questions he is trying to form.

The distance between the two vehicles has reduced.

Simon continued to gain ground, but only inching closer. Without warning the car in front accelerates and this increases the distance between the two in seconds.

Both cars pass Sweetslade Farm in a blur. Then the quarry works, Farmington Natural Stone is left behind as both cars maintain one hundred and ten miles an hour.

Simon is finding it difficult to keep control of his foot muscles and is closing his eyes repeatedly. His foot spasms and it slips from the accelerator and the car slows. He forces it back onto the pedal and it roars back up to speed.

They take a left-hand bend at high velocity. Ahead the road appears straight as an arrow for some considerable distance. Simon grits his teeth in determination.

As the car ahead straightens its trajectory, Simon closes his eyes and doesn't re-open them. His muscles seize and cease functioning.

The car veers off across the opposite carriageway, bursts through the hedgerow of trees and bushes and travels completely through the vegetation exiting it through the far side.

The tyres catch in the earth and the car rolls three times before ending up on its roof. All is still for a moment. The car explodes in a fireball, lighting up the surrounding countryside.

Meanwhile the other vehicle has slowed before coming to a halt some two hundred yards ahead.

The white reversing lights come on and the car retraces its steps all the way back to the exit point in the hedgerow. Two people get out and walk towards the gaping hole.

They both watch the conflagration, mesmerized by the spectacle. They hold hands. Then turn towards each other and begin to kiss and explore each other with their mouths and hands.

The car explodes a second time. Their passion escalates.

25th December 2016

08:15am

'I don't think I've ever felt more alive than I did at that moment last night.'

Penny covered Josh's hand with one of her own. They were both sat up in bed having a second cup of tea that Josh had brought in a few moments earlier.

He had prepared smoked salmon and scrambled egg for breakfast at seven forty-five.

'I concur Mr Styles,' she said and smiled broadly.

Josh turned his head.

'Although the cake is only half baked.'

'True. But can we forget that for today? Just let it be the two of us?'

'I concur Mrs Styles.'

They kiss.

Despite the lateness of the hour, they had returned home, they had both been wide awake before seven.

'Although.'

'Yes Penn?'

'I would like to hear how you left the situation with Suzi Fortesque.'

Josh smiled broadly.

'Dangling like a marionette. She won't lose any sleep over Simon's death, quite the opposite. I'll leave it for today, as you say, just the two of us. Then perhaps Jason Puddiphatt can give her a call on Boxing Day and set up phase two.'

'I was thinking of a staged mock suicide. *Can't live without the love of my life.* That sort of thing.'

'I love the way your inventive mind works.'

'Then with Suzi out of the way they'll be no one who can identify you or link the two of us together.'

'Simon's accident is bound to be on the local news at least. *'Tragic death of devoted family man and all that shit."*

Penny smiled.

'He was so entitled and cock-sure of himself. It never entered his head that he was being played.'

Penny turned and looked directly into Josh eyes.

'We must plan every one of our little adventures as meticulously as we have this one. Cover all eventualities so there are never, ever, any nasty surprises, again.'

'Absolutely. So, after Suzi have you had any thoughts on where next?'

Penny smiled and under the duvet moved her right leg so that it lay across both of Josh's while half laying on him. She brought her face up close to his and she draped her right arm across his chest and began playing with his ear.

He smiled.

'Would I be correct in assuming that your thoughts regarding the next target are, beginning to turn you on? Clearly earlier was not enough.'

'You'll be aroused when I reveal who I have in mind. Although I think you can guess.'

'Are you suggesting for one moment that I have an insight into your troubled, creative way of thinking?'

Penny smiled and lowered her eyes, before she kissed Josh passionately. She pulled away, the kiss still lingering between them.

'I'd be mortified if you didn't,' she said.

Josh smiled back and returned the ferocity of the kiss.

'Well, that is very audacious Mrs Styles. You do have panache I must say.'

Penny's right hand disappeared beneath the covers.

'You have a certain something yourself Mr Styles. What do you think of my choice of mark?'

It will be the most difficult to achieve, to date.'

They kissed.

'Faint hearts never won fair lady.'

They kissed, more passionately.

'It will require military level planning and execution.'

They probed each other's mouth with their tongue.

Josh began to trace his hand across Penny's body, before it disappeared beneath the covers.

'We cannot leave anything to chance.'

The duvet began to rise and fall.

Serial Killers

'We must allow enough time to pass to alleviate any suspicion,' gasped Josh.

'That would be a wise precaution,' Penny panted.

Both were breathing heavier, a flush appearing across their skin.

'So, George and Rivka Venton it is.

'It is so rewarding sharing an interest, *a folie a deux* as the French say,' Penny said.

'I think it brings us closer together,' Josh grunted.

They both disappeared beneath the duvet.

Follow Gary and his work here:

Serial Killers

HAVE AXE, WILL TRAVEL

BY

ANTHONY M. CARO

Serial Killers

"I don't think you should be doing this, Ellie," Sheriff Gideon said as he leaned back in his chair in his dusty office.

"Eleanor," spoke the former Ellie.

"Miss Eleanor."

"Miss Silas. Although you can call me Eleanor."

"Miss Silas Eleanor," the Sheriff slurred with an 1874 wiseacre drawl. "I don't think this is a good story for a journalist of your type."

"Because I'm a woman? You judge my journalistic talents because I'm a fairer?"

"No, reading and writing skills are rare in New Mexico territory. Make with your skills what you can," Sheriff Gideon said, filling his stereotypical western glass with equally stereotypical rye whiskey. "The story you're chasing might not be something you want to hear."

Eleanor kept one eye on the Sheriff, with one hand grasping a pencil and the other hand on her jotter, known today as a notepad.

"You drink?" asked Sheriff Gideon.

"Certainly not." Eleanor took severe offense at the statement that undercut her temperance sensibilities.

"Rarer." Sheriff Gideon let the word hang in the air. "You toss in bed at night, fretting over sins?"

"No, sir, I have no reason to keep from sleeping soundly." Eleanor intended not to let the Sheriff run her out of town.

"No sins?"

"Everyone sins."

"Y'all, believe in God?"

"Yes." Eleanor had to hide her indignation at such a question.

"And Moses? And Angel Gabriel?" Sheriff Gideon persisted.

"Sheriff, I'm here to interview you."

Sheriff Gideon sipped some more rye whiskey and let it swirl in his mouth before asking, "You believe in the hereafter?

"Of course I do."

Sheriff Gideon stared at her with his half-dead eye and cautioned, "You don't know what you're here after."

"I am here to report hard facts— I didn't come all the way to New Mexico to spin tall-tale yarns. I came here to report the news." Rarer still for an old west newspaper reporter. Many old west newspaper stories were made up inside jokes to amuse fellow newspaper brethren. Eleanor took her profession and herself seriously, even if the sheriff didn't.

Sheriff Gideon smirked as more rye whiskey meant fewer inhibitions.

"You stopped in New Mexico on your way to California for the gold rush story. Oh, yes'um, I have a telegraph fellow in town, too." Sheriff Gideon liked to wait between sentences to see if he could rattle Eleanor. "I read you plain. You didn't stop here to tell a Thunderbird story. You can make that up at home."

"I want to talk about the bounty killer." Eleanor's direct statement left Sheriff Gideon a bit rattled.

"If you believe in God, then I infer you believe in the devil." Sheriff Gideon appreciated deflection, so it seemed.

"Sheriff," I want to talk about the bounty killer. Not the Almighty. Not the Devil."

Sheriff Gideon held the whiskey glass in his hand and made wrist-twist circles with it, swirling what was left of the whiskey.

With a quick snap, the Sheriff shot down the last of that whiskey down his throat. "I'll split the trail with ya. The Almighty won't fit in if we talk about the bounty killer. But you can't talk about the bounty killer unless you're talking about the devil."

Eleanor took her turn, leaning back in her chair.

"You're going to spin yarns about the devil's bounty hunter reaching out and from down below and pulling the worst of the outlaws down to hell in blood-soaked revenge. Sheriff, I'm not from Tombstone. I said I don't spin stories for whimsy or profit."

"Maybe not whimsy." Sheriff Gideon's mind drifted as he looked at the now-empty whiskey glass. "You report the news?"

"As far as a telegraph will take it."

"Telegraph can go straight to hell, and I don't mean that as an insult. I mean it plain as dirt."

"Plain as dirt, are you saying the devil rips outlaws running from the law apart and drags their bodies to hell?" Eleanor asked the question contemptuously as she scribbled notes on her jotter. The contempt extended to tall tales posing as news.

"No, plain as dirt, I'm saying the devil gets their souls. Don't need the bodies. Same with heaven." Sheriff Gideon reached for the two-thirds empty bottle of rye. "They're not ripped apart, either. They're hacked, sliced, and cut up. The devil gets those souls whether the owners take a bullet in a shootout, die in their sleep, or get hacked with an axe. The devil don't need the bodies. Only the bounty killer does."

"Why?" Eleanor pressed her pencil tip on her jotter, expecting to hear the motive.

Sheriff Gideon's scoffing laughter filled the near-empty jailhouse. "To collect the bounty. When somebody's wanted dead or alive, you can't walk in here and say, 'Oh, I killed 'em, where's my $500?' No, you have to bring a body. But you don't need to bring the body."

Serial Killers

"Excuse me?" Eleanor looked up from her jotter, not following Sheriff Gideon.

"You need proof the outlaw's dead. Not a body." Sheriff Gideon spoke to himself when he said, "You should have seen the look on his face."

"Whose face? The bounty killer?" Ever the journalist, Eleanor needed clarification.

"No. Bloody Bart's."

"The cattle rustler?"

"Cattle rustler. Gunslinger. Killer. Now, ex-cattle tustler, ex-gunslinger, ex-killer, ex-Bloody Bart. I will not forget the look on his face when I stared into that bucket."

"Bucket?"

"I had to look in the bucket to see his face. That's where his head was."

Eleanor couldn't hide her annoyance at Sheriff Gideon's disrespectful attempt to spin an old-west yarn. The annoyance faded from her face when her journalistic skill told her he was not spinning yarns.

"Wanted Dead or Alive. As a journalist, you're not supposed to put anything in the record without verifying, right?" Sayeth Sheriff Gideon.

"No, I am not," Eleanor retorted.

"Lawmen, too. But I had my suppositions. I reckoned dead meant shot with a .45. Never thought he'd kill them with an axe. That was when I thought he was fighting against the devil's hordes, not that he was part of them. I should've shot him then and there. If anybody asked me why, I'd have made up some Thunderbird borrowed story about why I did it when he brought the bucket into the jailhouse. Same with the man whose head it belonged to. I should've shot Bloody Bart the three times I had the chance, but I didn't pull."

Eleanor heard a pained regret in Sheriff Gideon's voice. She scribbled a note about it on her jotter.

“I'd appreciate it if you kept that out of the story." Sheriff Gideon continued telling his version of events, although the legal record drifted toward a confession. I believe the Lord felt he needed Old Testament justice. Dead is dead. Maybe the Lord also smites in mysterious ways. Course, that's how I thought when I believed the almighty sent an avenging and plumb-useful angel. Never supposed I was dealing with one of them fallen angels.

Eleanor looked up from her jotter, expecting to see something other than a stone face from Sheriff Gideon. She had enough reporting experience to know a liar when she saw one. The look on his face? He's not spinning a yarn.

"Did the bounty killer have a name?" Eleanor asked the question she should have asked earlier, not so much for accuracy and clarity but to jar herself out of her shock.

"Didn't ask."

"You just gave him the money?" Eleanor had a way of framing her incredulousness at the tale as a legitimate reporting question.

Sheriff Gideon slightly sneered with the reply, "Was I supposed to converse with him? Read him the Bible?" He reached for the rye bottle and put more whiskey in his glass. "Maybe I should have read in the Bible. Not that it would have done any good."

"What did you do with the head?" Eleanor returned to reporter duties with the question.

"Buried it."

"You didn't try to arrest him?" A fair question from Eleanor. "You just let him walk out of your jailhouse?"

Sheriff Gideon's sneer shifted to outright laughter. "Arrest him on what charge? Wanted Dead or Alive's court scribble law talk, which, in plain lingo, means dead or alive. He brought him in dead. Dead is dead. No judge, lawyer, senator, or congressman scribbled down any particulars about rules with regards to how they got dead."

"No guilt?" Eleanor's question belonged on the editorial page.

"Yeah, for three days."

"What in blazes…" Eleanor blurted out the words but shifted in her saddle when the Sheriff's eyes narrowed in offense. She rephrased her words. "What on earth could make you lose sinner's guilt over letting that mad dog bounty killer walk out your door?"

"Brass Knucks Warren," the Sheriff couldn't look Eleanor in the face as he brought the whiskey glass to his lips and sipped. "Brass Knucks Warren on my mind, that's why. He was one of the worst.

"Was?"

"Was."

"You finished him?"

"I didn't. He took care of things." Sheriff Gideon crossed his legs and glanced at his old, worn, dulled spurs. The spurs lacked visual appeal, but looking at them kept him from looking at Eleanor. "Mad dog he is. Was.

I don't recall Brass Knuckles Warren sparring old men and people in banks begging for their lives. Or doing what Warren did to the women he took out of the bank." Sheriff Gideon tightened his grip on the whiskey glass before concluding, "Sometimes you got to sic a mad dog on somebody."

"Ever think of retiring, Sheriff Gideon?" Eleanor didn't express all her thoughts about Sheriff Gideon with the short statement, but the brief statement still expressed all her thoughts. “Doesn't seem like you're up for the job.”

"I guess you'll put that question into your notes with your not-very-journalistic of you in your story." Eleanor scribbled Sheriff Gideon’s notion.

"News. Not stories,” Eleanor never skipped a chance to correct Sheriff Gideon like she never missed a scribbling beat.

"Here's more news for ya," Sheriff Gideon said, downing the rye in the glass. "I was a great shot for the cavalry until I caught a rebel bullet. More than one. One may not even have been from a rebel."

Eleanor let Sheriff Gideon speak, feeling a little out of line.

"A cripple's not taking down Brass Knucks Warren or his .36 Navy with the more than 36 notches on its handle." Sheriff Gideon placed the shot glass on his desk. The glass had no further use since he gripped the bottle with his right hand, a hand trembling in fear.

Eleanor thought his grip twitched in fear until she noticed the scar on his wrist, a war wound. "I guess he carried brass knuckles with him, too." Eleanor redirected the conversation.

"No," Sheriff Gideon replied, seeking to get the record straight. "They gave him a funny name for the four rings he kept on his left hand. He used them like brass knucks. Right hand for shooting, left hand for punching. Truly, left hand for show. He never hit anyone. Not men, anyway."

"Did he come back in a bucket, too?" Eleanor continued her note-taking scribbling.

"Satchel."

"Satchel?"

"No need for a bucket when you only bring back a hand, one with four rings on it." Sheriff Gideon let the words roll nonchalantly.

"He brought back the hand?" Eleanor exclaimed with shock.

"Most of it," Sheriff Gideon noted, "Some of it was missing."

"Chopped up?" Eleanor could see where the story was headed.

"No. Chewed up. Rings on the fingers, none on the thumb, so not much use for it." Sheriff Gideon thought long and hard before suggesting, "I guess he didn't have any jerky."

"How'd you know it was Brass Knucks Warren's hand?" Good journalists like Eleanor always seek confirmation.

"The look on his face revealed all."

"You mean you looked into the bounty killer's face and read his thoughts?" Eleanor couldn't believe a lawman would be so naive.

"No. I didn't take the bounty killer's word. He didn't say anything," Sheriff Gideon clarified. "And I didn't look into the bounty killer's face. I looked at Brass Knucks Warren's."

Eleanor could write the story herself, but Sheriff Gideon did it for her.

"The bounty killer sliced Brass Knucks Warren's face off and put it in the satchel."

Eleanor stopped jotting on her jotter to inquire, “How could a lunatic with an axe take out a crack shot outlaw?”

“Don’t know. I wasn’t there,” Sheriff Gideon admitted honestly. Bounty killers like to shoot renegades in the back. That might be where he axed them. I reckon he got Brass Knucks Warren and Bloody Bart while they were unaware.

When a man with an axe meets a man with a six-gun, the man with the axe should go down. Not as if he can dodge bullets, at least not 30 of them."

"30?"

Sheriff Gideon further clarified, "Six shots from five guns. The Fillmore Gang has five members to match five old wanted notices that have long gone uncollected. That's who I sent him after. I told him that was all I had for him. They're miles away. I reckoned he'd take the hint, get out of town, stay there, and not return. He can go back to his hell and let me enjoy mine."

"What does he look like?" Eleanor couldn't believe she hadn't asked such a fundamental question earlier, but her mind wandered since she had never heard such a fantastic story.

Serial Killers

Sheriff Gideon loosened the pinkie finger on the hand gripping the whiskey bottle. Elanor turned in the direction he pointed, seeing a wanted poster on the wall. The poster didn't name the man on the poster, but it did list a reward, a hefty $3,500. The reward had a single term: DEAD. Not "Dead or Alive." Dead.

The poster depicted a drawing of the bounty killer. Eleanor struggled with how to describe him.

"No scars. No snarks. He looks like a plain trail drifter." Eleanor shook her head in disgust, "How many other bounty killers shot down the average saddle tramp looking for him?"

Sheriff Gideon shrugged.

Eleanor added a scribble to her jotter, mustering the few words she could utter. "I guess you're happy you won't see that face again."

"Who says?"

Eleanor gave Sheriff Gideon a look that screamed, "You don't mean…"

“Like I said, they have telegraphs in hell,” Sheriff Gideon drawled. “The Fillmore Gang is the No More Gang.”

“You think that’s funny?” Eleanor's words dripped with rattler venom.

“No, what’s funny is, for a second, I wondered how he’s going to drag six carcasses all of them miles when he’s only going to drag the vitals.”

Sheriff Gideon opened a drawer in the desk out of Eleanor’s sight. He pulled something out and placed it on his lap. Eleanor didn’t need her professional abilities to know what he had on his lap.

“Sheriff Gideon, I…” Eleanor’s words stopped cold when she heard the door to the jailhouse open slowly.

“Sit still,” Sheriff Gideon warned her. “He has to open the door to my office and walk through.” Based on the sounds of the nearing footsteps, that would come soon. “All I got to do is shoot through the portal, and we’ll see if he’s a man or devil.”

Serial Killers

Eleanor didn't dare look behind her when she heard the office door swing open. Sheriff Gideon had only one word for her.

"Duck."

Sheriff Gideon pulled a .45 out from under the desk, as Eleanor jammed her head down between her knees. She heard six loud shots ring out. The shots preceded the sound of a body hitting the floor.

The smell of black powder filled Eleanor's lungs as she rose up from her seat to stare at Sheriff Gideon sitting behind his desk, a cloud of black smoke surrounding him.

Eleanor remained in her chair as she turned to eyeball the prone body lying on the floor, not moving.

"Guess he was a man," Sheriff Gideon concluded.

Eleanor's eyes stayed transfixed on the prone, unmoving body lying next to a hefty, red-stained sack emitting the foul stench of rotting body parts. Her eyes remained focused even when the body switched to moving. The dead man on the floor rose to his feet, dead no more.

Sheriff Gideon guessed wrong.

Eleanor sat frozen in her chair when the bounty killer reached into the sack and pulled out a bloody axe. He stormed past her to the front of Sheriff Gideon's desk. The Sheriff put up no fight. We welcomed the axe like a penitent. One overhead swing split the lawman's head in half, adding the heavy scent of red blood mixed with the black powder's sulphur.

Although Eleanor had no bounty on her head, the killer didn't need to collect one when swinging his axe. He neared Eleanor's chair, where the journalist awaited her soon-to-come fate. She bought herself a little time, saying, "I'm a news scribbler. I have to know."

Serial Killers

The bounty killer paused a half-second before lifting up his poncho to reveal a solid steel plate with dozens of bullet indentations, six of which were new.

“Look, here,” Eleanor blurted, turning her jotter around so the bounty killer could see what she scribbled. He didn’t need to know how to read, as he saw a drawing of himself slinging an axe in the foreground with a lawless town as a backdrop.

The bounty killer knew how to read. He understood what the words scrawled on the pad said.

“The Axe-Slinger Cuts Down the Lawless!”

The bounty killer swallowed what he saw. He read those lurid old west paperbacks, too.

“You don’t need to go through all that trouble collecting bounties or dealing with double-crossing partners,” Eleanor stammered with fear. “I mean, I could help you spin your story. I can weave a good yarn with some god-fearing fire behind my pencil.”

The bounty killer contemplated what she said. He had been at this for a long time. He was tired.

With a simple nod of his head, he started walking towards the door.

Eleanor grabbed up her things and followed.

Follow Anthony and his work here:

Serial Killers

DIARY OF THE RED SPIKE

BY
MATT MARTINEK

Serial Killers

Human blood, once outside the body, will freeze at minus 3 degrees Celsius, which is slightly colder than the freezing point of water. A layman would not know this. But I am not a layman. I'm not a scientist, either. I am that which cannot be defined.

The beginning…the true seed to my story, does not have to do with a simple definition or scientific fact. It is much more complicated than that. After all, tragedy, in itself, has so many layers. The day that those towers, along with my life, fell into the earth, was a turning point…a true fork in the road for my psyche. My wife, Carol, worked on the 102nd floor of building 2 as an insurance agent for the AON Corporation. The impact zone from the airplane encapsulated floors 77 to 85. Obviously, she did not survive.

Most parts of that day I cannot remember, at least not in any worthwhile clarity. Shock is a funny thing. The last moments of normalcy I had were spent in my classroom (where I taught 5th grade English) with my eyes glued to the television screen as the events unfolded. The din of the children grew and grew, with some of them calling my name as they looked for some source of comfort or reassurance that things were still OK.

I instead provided them with a spectacle as I lost consciousness and passed out to the floor, upon the realization of my wife's location at that very moment. Things were not OK. And never again would be, for anyone.

The flyer with her photo was posted everywhere, along with all the rest. *MISSING*. That's what it said. After a little while, I wanted to replace them all with a revised version that read *DEAD. PURE, FUCKING, DEAD. MY WIFE IS DEAD*. I admired the families who held out hope. You know…the hope that somehow, one day, their lost loved ones would just show up at their doors, unscathed. Unfortunately, I did not have the strength for such a thing. I retreated into myself, into the apartment that now seemed much too large and frightening for a one-person show.

The remnants of my wife could only be found in those living quarters that had become my prison. I did not clean. I did not tidy up. I wanted it to be just as we had left it that day, as we rushed hurriedly to our all-important jobs, nearly knocking each other over as we scurried out the door.

Serial Killers

Ah…those moments that we threw away as if they didn't matter. But, oh, they did! Ignorance is bliss, or so they say. We did not even share a goodbye kiss. How pitiful is that?

I never went back to work. Couldn't bring myself to. I relied on our nest egg, which, thankfully, was not meagre, to make it through those lonely months, locked in that makeshift shrine. I left the apartment for the occasional grocery trip or to make sure my car still started, but that was about it. The rest of my time was spent trying to reclaim the past by looking at old photos, burying my face into my wife's dirty laundry that she had left behind, and occasionally spraying her Chanel No. 5 in our bedroom as I tried to remember what it felt like to be whole. The evenings were never kind. My nightmares shifted back and forth. One night, I would see her burning alive and melting into the floor as she sat at her desk, busy with an insurance call, and the next I would see her making the fateful leap out of the window and plummeting to the ground below as she wailed into the heavens. I always preferred the latter. Every once in a while I would be allowed to enter the dream and swoop down like Superman to save the damsel in distress. The reality of her demise, however, would never be known to me in my waking moments.

I fell, further and further, into the darkness. Pain turned to anger, and anger into hate. But what was I to do with it? I did not know. What I did know, however, was that a man has certain needs. Though I no longer had my wife, my sexuality remained intact and began to nag at me with a forcefulness I could not ignore. I longed…not for a relationship, but for the simplicity of a woman's touch…that same touch that I had taken for granted for so very many years. Interestingly enough. On September 11th, 2002, on the one-year anniversary of my loss, I decided not to attend the memorial service that was planned for the multitude of victims. Instead, I led a prostitute into my apartment, with the intent of doing whatever I wished, for as long as I would wish it. Love? Of course not. Just sins of the flesh.

It was not a proud moment for me, doing such a thing, but I felt that I had no other option available to me. Amber (as she wanted to be called) made the initial introduction as painless as she possibly could. She could tell that I was nervous as I approached her on the street, nearly shitting my pants as I cleared my throat and began to speak. She patted the crotch of my jeans with her palm before I could get out three words.

I immediately laughed at the gesture, and she snappily replied…"Oh, honey, it will be OK…don't be so uptight. This is about fun, right? So, let's make it that way." With an icebreaker like that, my worries were put to rest. And, strangely enough, there was no pimp or handler in sight, which made it even easier still. We made the five-minute stroll over to my apartment building and descended the stairs to the third floor, where the shrine to my previous life would be forced to accept an actual visitor.

As we entered the apartment, I was able to focus a little more on the woman that stood before me. Underneath a streetwalker's clothing and layers of badly applied makeup was actually a very pretty girl. About the height of my late wife, blonde (though I think it was dyed), and quite an athletic build. Her tanned legs really caught my attention as they sprouted from her short pleather skirt. I was chomping at the bit when she immediately soured the mood terribly.

"So, your wife at work or something?" Amber pointed to a framed picture of Carol and I on the wall, with a smart-ass look and smirk on her face.

“No, not at all. My wife passed last year, in the towers.” I spoke in a cold, flat, unemotional tone. Now was not the time, Amber.

“Oh my God, I’m so sorry! I didn’t mean to…”

“It’s perfectly fine. Honest mistake. I’m sure you get that a lot…you know, men cheating on their wives and such. Par for the course, I would assume. After all, men are pigs.” I took Amber by the hand, over to my couch, where I began to disrobe her. She kept looking towards the bedroom, but I wasn’t having that. There was no way I was going to disrespect my marital bed.

I would say that it was a bit animalistic as I devoured this woman sexually. A missing year of intimacy is no small thing. She…was not prepared. There were moments of pain on her part, but moments of pain for me as well, as my thoughts raced back to the love of my life and how much I missed her. One moment, however, changed the game completely. In the midst of my thrusting, I looked down at Amber’s face and instead saw nothing but my wife…only for a moment. Carol’s face then quickly disappeared.

I lost myself and wrapped my hands tightly around Amber's throat. I squeezed as hard as I possibly could. "You…are NOT MY WIFE!!!" I remember tears streaming down my face before I blacked out. This is what I did with all that pain. I had decided.

I woke up with my face sunk into a puddle of saliva that had collected on Amber's quickly bluing breast. I fell off the couch, startled, and retreated into the bedroom, slamming and locking the door behind me. Like a child, I jumped into the bed and yanked the covers over top of me, scared of the monster who lurked outside the door. I didn't want to believe it, but I knew that the monster was real, and it was one of my own creation. All of that pain…all of that anger…was let loose on this poor woman whom I didn't even know. After an hour or two (or more, I wasn't really sure), I gained enough courage to unearth myself and slowly open the bedroom door. Some naïve part of me expected to find an empty couch, and for me to realize that it was all just some delusion or bad dream. As the old door creaked open just enough to for me to see Amber's nude, discolored leg hanging down off the couch cushion, I slammed it shut once again. It was real. I fucking killed her.

To observe a human body after death is not something an uninitiated person can handle mentally. The color, the bloat, the mess that is expelled…I was not prepared for such a thing. I couldn't bring myself to even touch her. I simply watched, day after day, as her body began to change. As her stomach swelled and she began to stink, however, I knew that I had to do something. My freedom depended on it. And so, after a trip to the hardware store, I began to take her apart, piece by piece. She fell away, slowly, onto the tarp I had placed on my kitchen floor just for the occasion. I was 14 again, dismantling a foetal pig in biology class. The entire time, though, through all of the cutting and all of the sawing, I expected the police to bust down my door at any time and take me away. But they never showed. Hell…the phone that was in Amber's purse never even rang once. It was like no one gave a fuck about her…like she never even existed to begin with. She was the perfect victim.

Over the next two weeks, I drove pieces of Amber and her personal effects all over New York, being careful not to leave anything within 25 miles of my apartment. Feet were thrown off of bridges in the middle of the night, arms and legs dispatched into dumpsters hiding in unassuming alleyways.

The head was buried off a trail in Bear Mountain State Park. You get the idea. After the final pieces had left my possession, I felt strangely proud of myself for being able to pull it off. Excited, almost. There was one thing I did keep, however. Amber's blood. I collected every drop that fell. I could have dumped it down the toilet, or poured it down the kitchen sink, nice and easy. But I didn't. I kept it in my fridge instead, neatly collected into eight sealed, equally filled Mason jars. I wasn't even sure why.

Days passed, though my hatred did not dissipate. I was hoping, somehow, that through the murder I would be able to put my demons to rest, but I was wrong. And every day, whether I would find myself making a sandwich or getting a glass of milk, my eyes would wander to those shiny crimson jars of blood that I kept. I started a ritual of removing them from the fridge and stirring the contents, as I noticed that a kind of separation began to occur. It became some sort of sick, morbid fascination. Somewhere, in the deepest recesses of my mind, I appreciated the situation Amber had afforded me, and I did not want to forget her. As we all know, blood is everything.

I wanted nothing more than to shout out at humanity, maybe even to God himself. I wanted them all to notice my pain and to realize that I existed. MY pain should be THEIRS. Lives didn't really mean anything to any of them…just a multitude of tiny ripples, sinking into the beach. My late wife's memory was nothing more than wet sand, to be walked upon by the ignorant. But maybe, just maybe, I could make them see differently. If they knew that there was a monster among them, in plain sight, they would learn to appreciate the gift that they had. I wanted more, and more is what I was set on taking.

For whatever reasons, my thoughts kept returning to an old idea I had come across from long ago. I had seen it on the television late at night when I was a teen…the idea of some of these hitmen actually trying to devise a bullet made from ice that would make the tracking of their weapons completely impossible. In my situation, I needed something exactly like that. The ice would melt, leaving no trace whatsoever. After a while of running it over in my mind, I truly believed that this could be the path. But it would not be a bullet. It would need to be a little more personal. And a little easier to fashion. I wanted something quick, practical, and violent.

The method that seemed to make the most sense to me was to create some sort of knife or severely pointed object to create the fatal blows. And so, I began to experiment. I ordered a small deep-freezer and a home kit for latex Mold-making. Within a week, they were delivered straight to my apartment. Obviously, I had no idea what I was doing at first, but I was intent on learning. The test pieces went terribly. I first used a kitchen knife to make the latex form for the ice weapon, but the product that came out was much too fragile. No way that it would kill a person.

I then made another Mold, using a motorized sanding tool to form the hardened latex cavity into a knife-like shape, though somewhat thicker than before. Again, though, it was simply too weak. I was using a watermelon to test the hardness. I figured, if the ice could pierce the watermelon, it could pierce flesh easily. What I was making didn't even come close. The ice shattered to the kitchen floor with each attempt. I was stumped.

One evening, as I was pacing in my apartment, racking my brain about this little project I was embarking on, I realized that what I needed had been staring at me, right in the face all along. See, my father worked on the railroad for many, many years. Every so often, when he would hit a milestone of employment, the company he worked for would present him with an award for time served. And the award? It was usually a shiny, plated railroad spike, mounted to a varnished piece of oak. When my father died, one of his possessions that I took home was one of these awards, which now sat on a shelf in my current living room. A railroad spike was a perfect model for the weapon…thick and sturdy. I would simply have to make it a little sharper, that's all.

Unfortunately, though the spike itself was the perfect model, the frozen version of it still refused to pierce the watermelon. It snapped in half as I stabbed with it. I began to realize that maybe it wasn't so much the shape of the item, but instead the strength of the ice that I really needed to concern myself with. In my mind, ice was ice. It's ice if it's frozen at 10 degrees, and it's ice if it's frozen at below zero. Was it even possible to strengthen such a thing?

I nearly abandoned the idea altogether, until I came upon an article online that described, in detail, how to make ice nearly as hard as concrete. To my amazement, I read that if you add a certain amount of sawdust to the water that you want to freeze, the frozen product will be remarkably strong. They refer to it as *pykrete*, and it has been used experimentally for years, especially in arctic climates. I quickly found out that this was no myth. The frozen spike now pierced the watermelon with ease. I had done it.

I ran the situation over in my mind time after time. The victims would be random. No preferred type, only preferred location. Ah, the nonsensical killings of a god. I would troll the streets and back alleys of New York, with my weapon in tow, waiting for an opportunity. I had purchased gripped mechanics' gloves to negate slippage of the spike, and even a small briefcase for carrying it, that I had outfitted with insulation to prevent melting. I was so excited to begin the process, but then it happened. I opened my refrigerator door, and there they were. The jars full of Amber's blood. It hit me at that very moment. There was a reason why I had saved them after all. It was not to be a spike frozen of water. It was meant to be a spike frozen of blood. Amber's blood. She was still with me.

I had to do a bit of experimentation, of course, but I was still able to reach the same result as far as the practicality of the weapon went. The temperature of the freezer needed adjusted, as did the sawdust ratio, but that was to be expected. I did a test run of the blood spike, and it popped right into the watermelon without hesitation. But, this time, I needed to retain the ingredients used, as I had only so much of Amber's blood in storage. I did not want to waste a single drop. Each spike, as I figured, would take a little less than one jar of blood, which gave me room for about nine kills. More than enough to make my point. I could only imagine the police attempting to solve the riddle that I was about to present to them. Time yields results, and the answers I uncovered were far more than adequate. I was finally ready.

Stalking is an art form. I made a couple of dry runs over the course of a few days, just to practice. I would tail someone for a little while, trying to get as close as I possibly could before I was noticed. Honestly, it's a lot tougher than you would think. I was slapped by a woman in Times Square, when I broke that all-important space bubble of hers. Called me a "pervert," too. I did my best to keep my cool with her, as any unwanted attention was not any goal of mine.

But it was important training, and I took it seriously. Chess is a game of planning and forethought and wasn't designed for children.

The weekdays are for practice, but Sundays are for the big game. Admittedly, I was nervous. More than nervous…I was literally shaking. I wasn't sure if I could go through with it, but before I knew it, it was 8 PM on an unseasonably warm October night, and I was leaving my apartment with my briefcase in hand and murder on my mind. I chose Hell's Kitchen for my first foray…the vibe, the filth, and the alleyways made for an atmosphere ripe with opportunity. I parked my aging Chevy, took a deep breath, and exited the vehicle. I caught one last glance of my face in the driver's side mirror before I shut the door. Another fork in the road…a before, and an after. I would never be the same again. I sauntered about, away from the more popular avenues, looking for my perfect victim. About thirty minutes in, I was already becoming impatient. Lamplight was the enemy, and I couldn't spot one person leaving its glowing embrace. My footsteps became heavy and sweat formed on my brow. I began to question myself, and in a near panic, I turned around and began to make the trek back to my car, defeated. A part of me was relieved, though. *Was it some sort of sign?* My heartbeat slowed. I was going home.

Sometimes in life, however, fate does intervene. I could have easily made it another 500 feet to my car and abandoned my grotesque plan for good. And I would have, too. But the man walking in front of me decided to change the direction of my story completely. He made a left. As simple as that. And I followed. His dress amazed me as we turned from the light into the dark alleyway…knee-length business overcoat, short-brimmed hat, not unlike what I was also wearing as I stalked my prey. Ironic, really. Robert Louis Stevenson and his idea of duality of man popped into my mind as my cunning Hyde followed a naïve Jekyll into the blackness. I stayed behind, and attempted to match the man's footsteps, treading lightly, heel-to-toe, until I needed to pick up the pace a bit and close in.

All was working well until I reached about two yards from the man's heels. I clicked the briefcase open to procure the dreaded spike, which, to this man, produced a sound as alarming as a gunshot. His head turned towards me as he poised for escape.

I lunged; the blood spike gripped firmly in my gloved hand. With the force of an airliner smashing into a skyscraper, my spike was planted firmly into this unknown man's throat. Just as the towers themselves…he, too…fell.

I dragged the body to the side of the alley and pushed it tightly against the brick wall. I left the man, who was still gurgling away, with the spike lodged in his neck and blood pouring from the wound.

There was not much coverage on the murder, except for the information that it was the stabbing of a man in his late 40's. I expected as such. But I did wonder what they had found when they got to the scene. Was the spike completely melted by then? Were they able to differentiate another blood source on the victim? And what of the sawdust? Excitement crept into my being as I imagined the authorities pondering over such a strange situation. But it was not a time for rest, no. I needed to build upon the first step I had taken, and that's exactly what I did. There was no going back. For the next few weeks, I terrorized the five boroughs with kill after kill, perfecting my ways as I went along.

I traded in the briefcase (much too clumsy and loud) for an insulated carrying case to attach to my belt that I had fashioned from an old pistol holster. I also added more sawdust to the blood mixture, as on one occasion the spike did snap in half as it met a poor fellow's spinal column. The number of victims grew, as did my reputation in the press. I can't take credit for the latter, unfortunately.

It was now the middle of November, and it seemed I no longer had the warmer temperatures of early fall on my side. The police had actual evidence to draw from, now…the blood spike itself. Apparently, the murder weapon did not melt away like I had planned. *Fuck! Too much sawdust, I'd bet.* They even showed a photo of the actual spike in the newspaper, which completely blew my mind. Even stranger still, this coincided perfectly with the discovery of one of Amber's arms at the landfill, which was all over the news. *Would they make the connection? Would they get closer to solving the riddle?* I was confident that they wouldn't. Well, at least not until I completed my final kill. Amber's blood was running out. I had just enough for one more example in pain.

Serial Killers

At the very height of my abilities, with excitement bursting forth in my chest, I set out on one last hunting trip. The point was nearly made, and the journey almost fulfilled. Blood for blood. Life for life. All taken with impunity, just as nature intends. I found myself this time in the middle of Greenwich Village, as a light snow was beginning to fall. I envisioned the stark contrast of the fresh blood as it sprinkled onto the newly white-dusted street. A medium-sized crowd was departing the Comedy Cellar on Macdougal Street.

I was hoping to catch a straggler who may have been within walking distance of their apartment. It was a little more brazen than I was used to, but I had scoped it out earlier in the day and had a feeling that I would be in luck. I walked amid the show-goers, and watched as they dispersed in different directions, taking their chug-a-choo breaths of smoke with them. Minutes passed, and the group became less and less…until there was only me and her.

I had the woman in my sights from the very moment she stepped foot on the sidewalk, mainly because of the fur-lined hood she flipped up over her curly red hair. It was an easily visible target.

And, as they all do, she eventually strolled right into the blackness, with a monster nipping at her heels. I approached, slowly and carefully. *Close…closer still…yes…that's it. Almost there, my love…* I was a spectre, floating up from behind, spike in hand, living in the darkness in which we had found ourselves. At the very moment before the ultimate climax, I noticed something peculiar about this woman…from my past. I paused dead in my tracks as I realized what it was…the scent that I was so very used to. Carol's scent. That damned Chanel No. 5.

Our life together flashed before my eyes for a moment, until the beautiful dream was broken into by a quick flash of light, coming from my victim. I had made a mistake. This woman, with camera in hand, warm from the comedy show she had just seen, snapped a photo of me, deep in my pleasures. But not just of me. Of the spike, as well. I clumsily tried to hide my face with my arm, spun around, and ran back to my car, slipping and sliding on the icy sidewalks the entire way. I chucked the spike onto a low rooftop as I went. It was far from a graceful escape. More like an embarrassing one. I retreated back to my apartment, using whatever darkness and side streets I could manage as cover. Then, I simply waited…for the inevitable.

By the next morning, it was all over. *The Red Spike*, as I soon became known, was apprehended, and the terror ceased to be. And yes, I do realize the further irony at play. It was the memory of my late wife that served as the catalyst, and it was that same memory that ended my journey. Nevertheless, although one victim short and one jar of Amber's beautiful lifeblood wasted, I still had accomplished my goal. MY pain became THEIRS. And now, it's YOURS, as well. Always remember…blood is everything. Never take it for granted.

Follow Matt and his work here:

THE CURIOUS LIFE OF A SERIAL KILLER

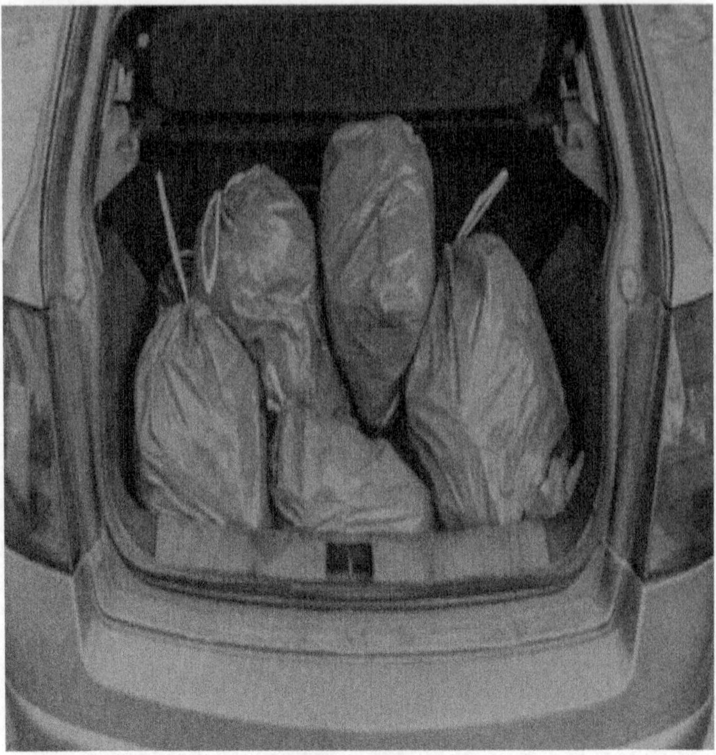

BY
DEL GIBSON

Serial Killers

Her heart felt heavy in my hand. Blood and matter dripped down my arm. When I tossed it into the bathtub it makes a squishy sound. My heart is pulsating with adrenalin. *I love this feeling, I'm in heaven.* The large knife I had grabbed from her kitchen slips from my wet fingers and stabs into the floorboards. The stench of blood mixed with fragrances from her broken bottles of perfume, lotions, and makeup, spreads a potent aroma around the bathroom at victim number 9s hovel of a flat in Takapuna, Auckland. It's tucked in amidst a row of townhouses that are attached to single car garages. From the state of the property, I could tell right away that her place was the pits; empty bottles of alcohol piled up in the recycling bin, the yard a tangled chaos of uncut grass, dead plants and overgrown trees.

When I picked her up on Karangahape Road, Auckland's redlight district, she was wearing a short black silky dress, purple high heel pumps, and a sparkling red purse slung over her shoulder – they're now ripped to shreds upon her bedroom floor.

Searching through her wallet, I took back the two fifty-dollar notes I'd paid the bitch for her time, and laid them flat on the vanity. I discover that her name is not Brittney, her real name is Cassie-Anne Williams. There's a public transport card, and an ANZ bank card under the same name. I drag her mangled body into the bathtub – she's heavy with death. Blood is splattered on all the surfaces, and the floor is slippery; I have to be careful not to skid and smash my skull on the corner of the bath or the loo. I'm naked having shucked off my suit shirt and black pants in her bedroom, so I wrap her pink robe around me that I find hanging on the back of the door, then shove the fifty-dollar notes into one of the deep pockets, along with her driver's licence which I'll keep as a memento. Her robe is a little small and it reeks of cigarette smoke and stank perfume. Suddenly ravenous (which is normal considering the energy I've exerted on this beautiful night of pure pleasure) I browse through her fridge, but it's empty except for a bottle of milk, and containers of leftover Chinese takeaways.

Earlier, I'd parked my Honda Prelude in the garage. I go through the internal door that takes me out to my car, where I collect my kill-kit from the boot; an oversized black army utility duffle bag. It holds the tools of my craft, several weapons, and cleaning supplies. After removing her robe and putting it into a bin liner, now the clean-up begins. I've almost perfected this part of the process. I've had a lot of practice with the other victims. I'd say I'm somewhat of an expert by now. Donned in a white disposable jumpsuit—because I know from experience that this is going to get messy—I hack her corpse into manageable bits and pieces with my Kabar knife, eviscerating the rest of her organs first. I pack the remains into black plastic bin liners. Then, methodically scrub the bathroom with bleach mixed with cold water, though, even with a mask on my face it burns my nostrils and stings my eyes. I proceed to wipe down any surfaces I know I've touched in the flat. I clean the knife I ended her life with, and I put it back in the knife block in her kitchen. After scrubbing my knife I used to dismember her with, I return it to the kill kit.

As I have a quick shower to clean off any remanence of the crime I just committed, a sense of relief and satisfaction rinses over me. *Each time I kill, another piece of you breaks away from me mother.* I carry the bags to my car and place them on top of the blue tarpaulin in the boot. I'll get rid of them before I get to Wellington, there are plenty of dumpsites along the way to choose from. I gather my clothes from my travel bag and dress as fast as I can. With my money and her driver's licence now in my wallet, I stuff the bloodied jumpsuit into the last rubbish bag, and tie it shut. Before I leave the flat, I douse all of the rooms, the garage, and my Honda with five canisters of vanilla air freshener.

It takes about an hour to drive from the North Shore down to Hamilton. It's nearing midnight by the time I find a hotel open at this time of night. Using cash, I rent a suite and sleep the night and day away in a discombobulated slumber, worried about the body in my boot. It's a risk, but I need to catch up on sleep because the thrill of the kill has drained me into exhaustion.

The next day, I reach Taupō and the sun is setting to my right. The landscape is drenched in golds and violets. While I'm travelling along the lake, all of a sudden, I hear a siren and when I look in the rear-view mirror I see a police car flashing it's red and blue lights.

"Fuck!"

I indicate and pull over to the left side of the road, hoping they'll pass by, but it pulls in right behind me. It's a male officer and he's alone. I think fast…if he searches the car, I'll have to take him out, but that will probably hinder my plans. Plus, killing cops is not my forte. But if it comes down to it, I won't let him take me in. I'll do whatever I need to do to get away. If I'm arrested, I'm toast. The wait is excruciatingly long; he must be running my plates. That's fine because I have several aliases that have worked well thus far. Though I know it's probably a random traffic stop, sweat bubbles on my brow, so I wipe it away with my sleeve. Admittedly, I am a little anxious because I haven't dumped the body yet. I inhale a deep breath and release a trembling sigh to calm my nerves. In the side mirror I watch him approach the car. I put down the window.

“Good evening officer, what seems to be the problem?”

“Evening. The reason I’ve pulled you over is because one of your brake lights is out. Can I see your driver’s licence please?” he asks, as his eyes do a quick sweep of the interior of the car.

My wallet is in the glove box. I grab my licence and hand it over. I’m praying to God that he doesn’t notice the black duffle bag sitting on the backseat. To me it looks like a flashing neon light, I’m hoping to him it looks innocuous.

“Where are you heading to?” He peruses my driver’s licence and hands it back.

“Wellington. I’ve got business there,” I reply.

“Well, have a safe trip. Get that brake light sorted ASAP.”

He tapped the roof of my car with his fingertips on his way back to his vehicle. I thank my lucky stars as he pulls away and carries on. *Fuck! That was way too close.* Slightly shaken, I continue until I find a private picnic area beside the lake.

With the perfect sized rocks I discover along the shoreline I then proceed to attach them with twine to all the bags; to ensure they sink.

Ten minutes later, I arrive at Huka Falls, where I wait until it's completely dark. When the last car drives off, I walk down the side path that I know has lighting, but it doesn't have any CCTV cameras. I know this because I've used this particular dumpsite once before, to dispose of victim number 5s remains. I carry the plastic bags to the water and chuck them one by one into the raging Waikato River. After I've finished, I travel on to Wellington, singing along to the radio. It's a long slow arduous journey because of the excessive roadworks along the way. When I finally arrive at my destination, I rent a motel room, and I have the best sleep I've had in weeks.

I'm in a club five days after my arrival in Wellington. This place sucks shit, but it's the best club I've found in this city so far. It's called, The Castle, and according to the Uber driver it's a staple here on Vivian Street. I like the fact it's underground; it makes me feel like I'm in a dungeon. The lighting is dimmed to an amber glow, allowing dark shadows to linger in the corners.

Its medieval vibe is interesting, as women walk around showing their tits as they deliver drinks on silver trays to some of the other patrons.

"What can I get you?"

"A shot of whiskey," I tell the bar-wench, when I plant myself on a rickety creaky bar stool.

Serial Killers

She looks sexy as hell tonight. There's a tattoo of a witch on her left shoulder blade – I hadn't noticed it on the previous night's I've been coming here. She was initially going to be victim number 10, but the fact she's merely the bar manager takes her off the list. I only target prostitutes and strippers. Why, you ask? Because they are hussies tempting hard working men to depart with their wages. It's all part of their cunning plan.

They get you drunk at the bar, make you hard and horny with their entertainment, and if you pay them the right amount, they'll flash their Brazilian waxed pussies as a teaser, and when they twerk their bouncing ass cheeks in your face, you feel like you've won the grand prize. When really, you become their prey, and them, the apex predators. If you are prepared to depart with a weeks' worth of wages, they offer additional services in the backrooms – so I've been told.

"That'll be six bucks, thanks," she says, holding out her hand, breaking me from my delicious thoughts.

I hand her a fifty dollar note and she passes back the change. I down the poison, it burns my throat, and it tingles inside my head, bringing me to a whole new level of consciousness. I find a booth close to the stage, and I sit in the semi darkness and wait. It's 8:30pm and the DJ's playing Portishead's, *Glory Box*, on the sound system. The club is filling up fast, are they all here to see the Three Magical Princesses too? Two heathens are dancing and writhing around poles, dressed in G-strings, sweat, and rancid perfume – I get a gust of it from where I'm sitting.

This is my third night in a row coming here, for me, it's a first because I never hit the same place twice. But tonight, I'm on a mission. The only reason I've returned is because of the Three Magical Princesses, who perform at 9pm, five nights a week. They're a sight to behold. Triplets. They'll be victims' numbers 10, 11, and 12.

At 9pm, the lights fade to black, and the music changes to *Lady Marmalade*, by Christina Aguilera. Suddenly, the stage explodes with colourful lights. When the princesses grace the stage, the audience erupts. Whistles and shouts carry above the music, but I block everything out so I can focus on my prey.

Serial Killers

Tonight, they're dressed in different outfits than the previous nights. They seem more vivacious and appealing. I'm in awe, when they appear dressed in similar and transparent sexy lingerie. The first princess is wearing a silver outfit that glitters in the lights, with silver tassels hanging from her nipples. The second princess is dressed in gold, golden tassels, gold makeup; she looks like Cleopatra. And the third princess is wearing diamantes that sparkle all over her body. They wear black bob cut wigs and tiaras on their heads. I know this because their hair is different from their previous shows.

I'm enthralled as they dance in circles, twist and twirl their curvaceous bodies into contorted angles, whip elegantly around the poles, rub themselves against one another, gyrating a perfectly choreographed performance. They crawl across the stage on hands and knees as groping men in the front shove handfuls of money down their G-strings. Some throw dollar notes and gold coins at their feet. The princesses own the stage and seem to shimmer like angels. They finish off their show by flashing their assets down below. The audience screams for more. I want them to shut the fuck up!

Over the course of two days, I've formulated a plan of sorts to divide and conquer. It'll be no small feat to destroy them one at a time. *I like a challenge.* A nasty headache is building behind my eyeballs, stabbing my temples, like it does right before a kill. I wait patiently by the bar because I know the princesses will come over for their free staff drinks like they've done the last two nights. The bar is emptying now the main show is over. The club is dank with the odour of stale beer and sweat, and the bar is sticky with dregs of alcohol when I lay my hands upon it. Whiskey is getting to my head, but I won't get drunk, or it'll defeat my purpose. I need to stay sharp and on form.

After some time, the princesses approach the bar. When they ask for their drinks, I swivel around on the stool and face them. They're dressed in long red flowing gowns that sweep the floor. As they shuffle in beside me, I get a waft of weed. Their tiaras are still affixed to their heads. Long blonde hair feathers around each of their shoulders.

I scoot closer.

"Great show by the way. Can I buy you lovely ladies a round of drinks?"

"Of course you can, and thank you for coming to the show," the first princess acknowledges.

"Name your poison," I say.

"Make it three Porn Star Martini's and we'd be very grateful," says the second princess.

"How very kind of you," the third princess chimes in.

I wave the bar-wench over and order the filthy sluts their cocktails. She concocts the ingredients on the bar in front of us. It is very interesting to see how fast she works her magic. They take their drinks and start chatting with the bar staff. A slow soft Jazz melody floats around the bar as the minutes drag by. The princesses giggle and drink, clinking champagne glasses with strawberries in them. Vaping dragon clouds swirl around them like cloaks.

"Another round, princesses?" I ask.

“No thank you, we’ve got a party to get to,” the princess closest to me replies. They collect their handbags from behind the bar. “You can come along if you want,” she says flippantly.

Too easy!

“We’re heading to a shrooms costume party, if you don’t mind doing magic mushrooms,” one of the princesses says with a crooked smile.

I can’t tell one from the other, being identical makes it nearly impossible to differentiate between them, especially when they’re dressed the same.

They giggle in unison, making me feel unnerved for some reason. *I’m going to wipe those grins off your fucking faces.*

“Excellent! Thank you, I have no other plans,” I reply, smiling like the Cheshire cat that caught the elusive mouse.

I hadn't anticipated this, it's turning out better than I had planned. Initially I thought I'd have to befriend one of them and then lure the other two in somehow. *I guess it'll make it easier for me to kill them if they're fucked up on magic mushrooms, then I can take them out at the same time.* I put my black leather backpack over my shoulders, which is heavy with my Kabar knife, 9mm Glock, and a box of ammo.

We exit the club, and I follow the princesses into a sleek black limo. Another four people clamber in after us, and I'm perched in tight between two of the princesses, while the other princess has her long legs laying across the lap of a man in a Captain Sparrow pirate costume. It's stuffy in here; claustrophobia is making me edgy, but at least the sunroof is open.

Three chicks dressed as zombies are standing up with half of their bodies poking out of the roof, with champagne bottles in their hands, making a show of themselves and carrying on like drunken idiots. *I hope they hit a bridge, decapitation, that would be a hoot!*

We're dropped off outside an enormous old Victorian house. *People are Strange*, by The Doors, is leaking out of the open windows. There are several people outside milling about, smoking, drinking and talking shit no doubt. As we enter the house, the princesses receive hugs and cheek kisses from the partygoers. Cannabis, cigarette smoke, and alcohol permeate the air. Incense sticks tickle my nostrils as I trail the princesses into the kitchen, where a Viking is leaning against the refrigerator talking animatedly with Frankenstein's monster. We huddle around the marble island counter.

"Have you got any brew left love?" one of the princesses asks the host, who's dressed as a Fairy Godmother. She's plump, with piercing purple eyes – she must be wearing contact lenses.

"Of course, my dears, just give me a moment." The Fairy Godmother walks over to the stove. "Help yourselves to drinks," she says, pointing to the fridge.

I decline a drink, but the princesses each grab a colourful beverage.

"How rude of us! We don't even know your name," one of the princesses says, as she glides in beside me.

The other two princesses' snigger. I feel my cheeks heat in anger; it's as though they have a secret language with each other that only they are privy to.

Before I have a chance to answer, the Fairy Godmother cuts me off. "Here you go. It's shrooms in hot chocolate, it makes it go down easier," she says, as she ladles us each a drink of the brown concoction into cups that look like skulls.

It makes me wonder if this is a Halloween party, even though it's only mid-July. We toast to a good night. I screw up my nose at the smell, and the taste of fungus against my lips makes me want to gag. I pretend to sip it to fit in, but not wanting to get wasted.

"I know, it's not very pleasant to drink, but it'll be worth it." The Fairy Godmother encourages me.

I shadow the princesses into the living room. We sit, spread around on couches and chairs, wherever there is room, and I place my black leather backpack on the floor beside my feet. That's when I notice the princesses extra-long manicured fingernails; they must be fake. Pink Floyds instrumentals is making my head feel fuzzy. The room is full of people dressed in elaborate costumes. A white Rabbit and Pennywise are dancing next to a Warlock and Little Red Riding Hood. The Priest from the Exorcist is making out with a Nun by the fireplace. The house is slightly rocking, like I'm on a boat out at sea. There are too many people, and the lights are too bright.

Feeling slightly sick, I ask Robin Hood squashed in next to me, "Where is the bathroom?"

"Up the stairs to the left," he slurs.

The mushroom drink must be having some effect on me, even though I merely touched it with my lips; it must be very potent. My legs are a little wobbly as I make my way up the stairs. I pass Michael Myers and a Troll cackling on the staircase. Someone in a Scream mask is toking it up with Chucky at the top of the stairs.

Fortunately, the bathroom is unoccupied. *Fuck! I've left my backpack downstairs.* I throw the rest of the shrooms down the loo, and splash cold water on my face to perk myself up. I'm beginning to think it was a really bad idea coming here. I'm way out of my comfort zone.

As I venture downstairs grasping the banister for balance, I can't hear any music. In fact, the house is as silent as a cemetery. Has the party already finished? How long was I in the bathroom? I'm confused, then stunned, when I enter the living room and it's empty. I go for my backpack but it's vanished.

"Hello," I yell, as I walk deeper into the bowels of the house. "What the actual fuck, where is everyone?"

I hear movement behind me. I go to turn…but I'm knocked to the ground and the world goes black.

When I drift back to reality, I'm tethered by a rope around my ankles, naked, and hanging upside down from the ceiling. My arms dangle free. I'm high enough that I'm face to face with the princesses and the Fairy Godmother.

Their eyes are so red, they look like they're bleeding. Their features are truly petrifying; lips red, dripping blood, and their faces are smeared with it. Then I see their fangs. *Vampires?* I piss myself and I can't stop quivering.

Over in the corner, piles of bodies are stacked upon one another. I see taffeta, fur, masquerade masks, crumpled bits of jewellery, ripped and shredded costumes smothered in mushy red fleshy bits. Blood is spattered on the walls, the floor, and entrails slide to the ground, organs and unidentifiable body parts turn the room a murderous red colour. The stench is so overwhelming I vomit all over the floor.

"What the fuck are you doing?" I scream out in horror.

A princess holds *my* gun to my left temple.

"Hmm…you thought you could kill us with this stupid thing?" She tosses the gun, and it destroys the wall. "We followed you the first night you came to the club. We can read peoples' minds; it's one of our gifts.

When we heard what you've been doing up north and that you intended to kill us too, we've been keeping an eye on you just in case you decided to act on your impulses. You're fucked in the head! You've been murdering prostitutes and strippers just because your mother abandoned you to become a drug addicted street hooker. Are you fucking kidding me?"

They come in closer, so all I can see are their piercing long fangs. They are beasts, pure and simple. Note to self: Vampires are not at all like they're portrayed in the movies, all sparkling and beautiful. No! They are not to be romanticised: They are monsters!

"You messed with the wrong people, or should I say Vampires," one of the princesses says, as her fingernails scrape my skin.

I plead, "I'm sorry, just let me go and I promise I'll never hurt anyone ever again!"

My eyes are shut tight, and I pretend to sob. I desperately need a way to escape, perhaps I can trick them in to letting me down?

I've never been more scared in my life, but it only makes me furious. I guess I'm angry at myself for believing that I could take all three at the same time. I became complacent and now I'm kicking myself for it. Fuck! *That's right, they can hear my thoughts. I'm screwed.*

"You don't have to do this. I'll stop if you let me go, and I'll leave town immediately!" I scream so viciously that my throat hurts, and I'm left trembling.

"It's not that simple. You're a beautiful young woman, you have your whole life ahead of you, and you're only twenty-six-years-old," the Fairy Godmother whispers in my ear. Her breath tickles my skin, making the hairs on the back of my neck stand on end.

"We'd probably understand if you were a male, you know, with mummy issues and whatnot," says one of the princesses. "It's not normal to behave this way, killing women in a vendetta against your mother. You have serious issues lady."

Blood rushes to my head, and it feels like I've been slammed with a wrecking ball. I'm too scared to open my eyes.

"The thing is, you've come into our territory, this is our domain. We don't give a fuck about the women you killed up north. That's your baggage, but you can't come here causing problems. You're a threat that must be eliminated."

When I open my eyes, I see the Fairy Godmother pull something from her apron. It's a silver piece of jewellery that she puts on the end of her finger. She pokes it into one of my arms. I don't feel the blood release from my body, but the sound it makes as it drips into the silver goblet she's clasping in her hands, churns the bile inside my gut, especially when I see the goblet passed around, and they drink my blood from it with a delicacy and grace. *They're fucking teasing me, heathens!*

"Yes we are, sorry. How uncouth of us, playing with our food."

Their giggles stab inside my head. I don't know, nor do I care who is saying what anymore. My arm throbs, and a headache thumps inside my skull. I hear a door open, and suddenly a male voice booms into my ears, it's so loud it resonates around the room.

"Stop this. Look at this mess!"

A handsome man in a pinstriped suit leans his head into my face. His skin looks like porcelain, and his eyes are pure black. The Vampires back away slowly, hissing at the man, with disappointment on their ugly faces. Though, a sense of relief overcomes me, now I know I'm about to be rescued.

"Help me, please," I cry, "they're Vampires and they're trying to kill me."

"Of course. You poor thing, you must be terrified," he says, but he doesn't move. Why isn't he rushing to release me?

"Please, hurry! I don't want to die this way."

"I'll let you down when we are finished with you." He spits his words in my face – smelling like death and decay.

I'm beyond fury by now, I want to rip off his head and spit down his throat. Wriggling and fighting back, all I can think about is making them suffer. If I can get to one of them, perhaps they'll back off and let me go? I need to complete my mission, otherwise it would have all been for nothing!

"You fucking brutes. How dare you do this to me, you better make it quick otherwise I'm going to kill you all, believe me," I shout an empty threat.

"Oh, you think so, do you?" the man replies.

When he breaks my left foot between his fingertips, then proceeds to quickly break my other foot, I scream out in excruciating pain. With a flick of his fingers, he shatters my kneecaps one by one. When he grabs my right arm, I semi pass out. I feel the essence draining from me as consciousness comes in and fades out like waves on the ocean. I feel their fangs sink into the fleshy parts of my body.

I stop breathing for a moment as my pain reaches its limits.

“You humans are ridiculous. You let one little incident ruin your entire lives, instead of dealing with your problems in the normal manner, like counselling, talking to someone, getting help. Instead, you decided to murder innocent women,” the Fairy Godmother yells in my face.

The man cuts the rope. When my head greets the floor, I hear something inside me break, knocking me out again. When I come back to the present, I’m lying on the floor next to the pile of dead bodies. The man is yelling. He sounds guttural and dreadful – it shoots shockwaves through me, snapping me alert.

“…*then* we’ll have to dispose of the bodies and burn the house down. You shouldn’t have killed all of those people, what the hell were you thinking?”

“We’ve been bored; it’s been years. We wanted to get to this woman, and the others were merely collateral damage. We can move away. We’ll go back to Rome, or perhaps we could go and stay with Gillian and Alex in Egypt?” I hear one of them say.

Serial Killers

Holding my breath, I'm pretending to be dead, since now they're distracted. It might work, if I keep quiet, I could escape.

The man says, "We can't just up and move you fools! We've made a life here. This is where we belong now. You murdered an entire house full of people to get to this one pathetic human being! I don't understand, I thought you were happy here?"

When I open my eyes to have a quick look, they turn as one in my direction. The man pounces and drags me across the floor by my hair. My head is bumping along the ground, and it hurts like a mother fucker. I look down at my body, and I'm missing my arms and legs. Unadulterated terror rips a hole in the fabric of my pitiful existence. With their deadly fingernails, they peel off my face. What is left of my body is convulsing in the final throes of death. Tears stream from my eyes, leaving the moment blurred.

I know I'm dying, so I guess God didn't have a purpose for me after all. My mission was a complete failure. But at least this part of my task is complete; I no longer look anything like my fucking pig of a mother. The last thing I see before the grim reaper takes me, is the man ripping my bloody beating heart out of my chest with his hand.

Follow Del and her work here:

Serial Killers

THE WATER IS LIFE

BY
JOHN DODD

"No signs of a struggle, no defensive wounds, victim was found sat up in their chair, held in place by their own clothing tied around them, initial autopsy suggests that they ingested too much water which resulted in a cerebral edema." Detective Inspector Alvarez put the photo of the latest victim on the board, "Owain Jones is the youngest of the victims by far, in good health, without any co-morbidities and a martial artist by his interest, he wouldn't have been easy to subdue."

"Eight in four years," Detective Sergeant Richards cast his eye over the other images on the board, "And if he's now picking healthy young men as victims, it suggests that he's got his technique down."

"They," Detective Constable Smith said, "They could be a man or a woman."

"Freaky Fucking weirdo," Richards replied, "I agree, it's not limited to men or women, what's the link between the victims, we need to stop *them* before they strike again."

“We’ve got a month,” Alvarez tapped the board, “They only kill on the days of the full moon,” She paused, “Unless they start to get bold with it.”

“Fucking Werewolf,” Richards snapped, “Only a werewolf would leave paw prints everywhere, this bastard’s a ghost.”

“And there’s no connections between the victims at all?” Smith asked. “They just all died the same way, nothing in common?”

“First multiple case?” Richards’ demeanour changed as he looked over at the young constable, “Arn is the first serial killer I’ve had to deal with, and I hope, the last.”

“Arn?” Smith asked, “We know their name?”

“No,” Alvarez moved down the board and pointed at an intricate tattoo from the autopsy, pointing at each of the victims in turn, “In every case, the victim has a fresh tattoo somewhere on their body, Arn usually leaves the cling film over it to preserve the pattern.”

"Why Arn?"

Alvarez tapped the tattoo, "This is the Nordic symbol that represents Arn, and as a norse goddess, she was responsible for dragging sailors down into the water to their deaths. We figure that whoever is doing this is fixated on that, for what purpose, we don't know."

"And there's no connections between the victims?" Smith frowned, "I mean, at *all*..."

Alvarez walked back from the board and sat down opposite Smith, "We've got more than a thousand images of the victims and the places where they were found, the only connection that I could see is that most of them lived untidy."

"Untidy?"

"Hoarders for the most part," Alvarez said, "Most of them liked getting a bargain at the car boot sales or the charity shops, and you spend long enough doing that without ever having a clean out, your place starts to look like a car boot sale."

“Think there’s any possibility that that’s why they were targeted?” Smith asked.

“I think if you’re targeting people for buying crap from second hand stores, the target environment is so rich that you’ll never get an idea of who’s next.”

“But what if that’s something to do with it?” Smith asked.

Alvarez smiled, not unkindly, “Tell you what, it’s your first day on the job, and as much as anything else, you need to get a grounding in what is and *isn’t* useful to focus on, so if you want to spend the day looking through the reports and photos, then have at it.”

Smith pulled the first box onto the chair next to his desk, the lid was dusty, but the contents pristine, within were reports of the first victim.

Adele Chambers, Retired, 80 years old, single, no relatives, lived in Wrexham

The pictures showed a house that had been submerged under the weight of possessions within it, more chairs than a king would need, under those chairs, more clothes than a queen would wear, and along the walls, dozens of collectable plates and artwork. The body was in a large armchair, the type that recline to sleeping when the occupant can't be bothered to rouse themselves.

Smith looked through the photos, nothing remarkable, nothing out of the ordinary beyond the body in the middle of the room, the tattoo on Ms Chambers hand still bearing the cling film on the top of it when the photos had been taken. Smith put the contents back in the box and opened the next.

Stanley Ovenden, Retired, 72 years old, single, no relatives, lived in Sheffield

Similar house, same sort of chair, the tattoo on the shoulder this time. Smith looked through faster this time, getting some idea of what Alvarez was on about. She opened the next box.

Mary Pinner, Cashier, 63 years old, single, two children, lived in Oxford, tattoo on the left hip.

Angelo Starosta, 61 years old, translator, wife, one child, lived in London, tattoo on the left hand

Dennis Wheeler, 54 years old, rail worker, boyfriend, no children, lived in Doncaster, tattoo on the back of the neck.

Emma Ludovic, 42 years old, teacher, several boyfriends, no children, lived in Margate, tattoo on the back of the left knee

Willa Stonehouse, 32 years old, chef, wife, no children, lived in London, tattoo on the forehead.

Smith sighed as he put the lid back on Willa's box, it had been a long day, even by patrol standards, where he'd come from, and his eyes hurt from staring under the harsh office lights. He flexed backwards in the chair.

Serial Killers

Serial Killers almost always had a pattern, something that tied together what they wanted to achieve, what they thought they were doing.

He thought back to the limited studies that he'd done in his training days, serial killers usually stayed well within a pattern of age or gender, and they usually had some sort of reasoning behind what they were doing.

What was the pattern to this…

Smith paused, opening the box again and looking through it, it had been in the background till her thought just then. One of the last images taken, Willa's house, and there, on the table near the chair where she'd been found.

What was that…?

A small green figurine, difficult to make out on the photo, but the pattern on the front looked to be the same as the tattoo on Willa's forehead. Smith opened Emma's box, no longer caring for the hour, looking through the images till he found the framing shot with Emma sat on her chair, the kitchen table in front of her, and on the table, at the back, near obscured by the stacks of unopened mail, something that looked a lot like the figurine.

Dennis, a figurine was in his bedroom, not near where the body was found.

Angelo, there on the window sill, part covered by the curtains

Mary, there it was, on the floor beneath the table, surrounded by other tat.

Stanley, behind the chair, next to the door

Adele, on the mantelpiece.

Smith looked through Owains box, the images there mostly digitised, and there, by his weights bench, the small green figurine. He zoomed in on the image, looking at the pattern on the front, same as the tattoo.

Had to be connected, it wasn't uncommon in primitive cultures to leave a representation of your gods in a place where you had won a great victory, what if the figurine held the answer to the riddle…?

Smith looked at the clock above the door, past nine in the evening.

It would keep till the morning…

Smith returned early, unable to switch off, he'd been up till the early hours chasing every wild goose on the internet. Functioning only through the chemical assistance of red bull infused coffee, he tried to look awake as Richards came in, looking for all the world like he'd had a peaceful eight hours and didn't have a care in the world.

“All nighter?” He looked down in amusement, pausing by his desk and reaching into the drawer, taking out a wooden box and placing it on the desk in front of Smith, opening it to reveal a perfectly arranged stack of Mars bars, “Coffee is fine, but if you don’t have something to eat, you’ll still crash in a few hours, these might keep you awake long enough to tell me what you’ve found.”

“Thanks,” Smith dipped into the box, the first bar disappearing in two bites.

“I get them cheap,” Richards pointed to bars, “Get in there, tell me about what you’ve found that’s kept you up all night?”

“There’s a figurine in the homes of all the killings,” Smith paused to finish the second bar, washing it down with the remnants of his rapidly cooling coffee. “it’s not always next to the body, but it’s always there.”

"You think the killer leaves one to mark the killing?" Richards looked down at the images that Smith had pulled the previous night. "You know, Owain was killed three days back, the scene will still be sealed, we could go take a closer look at the one in his place."

"Can we?"

"First tangible connection between all the murders," Richards took one of the bars for himself, dropping the box back in his desk, "I'm for following it up, you coming?"

Owains house was messier than the images had made it seem, the faint smell of mould even over the scent of death. They picked their way through the debris of Owains life, stopping at the place where his weights were, the only place where the floor was not strewn with other things, and underneath, the small green figurine. Smith put her gloves on and picked up the figurine, putting it in an evidence bag before taking a closer look. Unremarkable, old looking, a stylised wooden person with the pattern carved on the front of it. Smith turned it over and made to pass it to Richards, he held his hand up.

"Not my evidence," He said, "That's your win, take it, let's get it back to forensics and see what we can find out about it."

It was two days and late in the day when forensics returned the figurine, still in the bag that Smith had put it in, with a five page report to go with it.

"No time like the present," Smith leaned back in his chair and picked out the first page.

"You'll learn at some point," Richards said, "That all nighters rarely produce the best investigative work."

"I was sleep deprived when I thought of the thing that got us here," Smith glanced over as Richards shut his computer down and made a point of leaving his desk drawer open.

"Just in case you find you need more than coffee," Richards smiled, Smith's enthusiasm an unexpected high point in his day, "If you find something interesting, by all means give me a call, but only if it's before five."

"It's five past five now," Smith frowned.

"Look at that," Richards grinned as he took his coat off the back of his chair and whirled it over his shoulders, "Grab some sweets and go home, I'll catch you tomorrow…"

Smith waited till he was gone before pocketing two bars and putting the report in his bag, dropping the figurine in next to it. It wasn't protocol to take evidence out of the office, but he did his best thinking when he had the things he needed in front of him.

The report made for interesting reading, the figurine wasn't a cheap copy of something, but an actual antique going back some decades, possibly even centuries. Trace elements of various heavy metals suggested that it had seen a number of different climates, and there were elements of skin and secretions all over it, suggesting that it had been frequently handled, but the patterns on the front of it showed signs of being grooved recently, giving the lie to the possibility of it being ancient.

Unless someone just regrooved it…

Smith read the report again, then over the page of notes he'd made to add to the notes that he'd already put together on the all nightery. The figurine could be an effigy of Ran from many years ago, but something like that belonged in a museum, what would it be doing out there, how would all the victims have got hold of it? Most antique shops wouldn't know what they were looking for, and charity shops wouldn't stock something like that as the chance of reselling it wouldn't have been high.

But then those who like curios and the discarded weirdness of others may just find it fascinating…

He put the notes back in his folder before taking the figurine out of the bag and turning it around in his hands, taking his phone and shining the torch into the cracks of the pattern, trying to see if there was anything else in there.

You know you're obsessing when you think you're going to find something forensics haven't.

Serial Killers

The doorbell rang and Smith glanced at his phone, takeaway was early, but he wasn't going to argue that, and if he didn't get to the door quickly, one of her neighbours in the block would probably come out and claim it. He moved quickly to the door, unbolting it and pulling it open. The figure in the hallway wore a long green robe of heavy cotton, a large hook obscuring their face from the lights on either side, their hands held together in the sleeves of the robe.

That wasn't a delivery boy…

Smith's eyes went wide as there was a faint blast of air and he felt a pinprick in his stomach, reaching down to pluck the dart out quickly. His vision swam and he staggered back from the door, co-ordination lost, his legs feeling weak. The figure followed him in, closing the door and bolting it behind them. Smith crashed to the floor as his legs gave way, his lungs feeling heavy as the sedative took effect, hoping against hope that someone would have heard the crash.

Who was he kidding, the last time someone got killed here, the only response from the neighbours was yelling at them to stop interrupting coronation street.

Smith looked up, his vision dimming as the figure started to drag him further into the apartment.

He woke in her chair, a burning sensation both inside and outside his stomach, all his muscles cramping, his head pounding. He stirred, realising that he was bound to the chair by his belts and what looked to be securing straps, glancing down through blurred vision at his bloated stomach, the new tattoo covering where the dart had struck him. He tried to move, but the discomfort grew, his head feeling like it was splitting open. In front of him, the figure stood in silence.

“Don’t do this,” Smith winced in pain with every word, his heart pounding in his chest.

The figure said nothing.

"Why…?" Smith mumbled as he felt his vision blurring, a sudden tightness in his neck as he felt darkness closing in from all sides

The figure said nothing, turning to leave.

It was the next day when Alvarez and Richards came to the apartment to speak to Smith, working harder than you should was one thing, evidence and forensics reports going missing were something else entirely. Words needed to be had and witnesses would be needed to make sure that HR didn't have a field day with it afterwards. Alvarez knocked on the door, waiting a few seconds before knocking again. "Smith, it's Alvarez," She called, "Open up."

No response

Alvarez banged on the door again, "Come one Smith, open up."

No response

“Call him.” She said to Richards.

Richards dialled Smiths’ number, the sound of the phone ringing coming from inside the apartment, it rang till the call dropped.

“Again,” Alvarez nodded.

Richards called again, the phone ringing till it dropped the call again. “Car’s outside, phones in the apartment…”

Alvarez nodded to the door, “Open it.”

Richards reached down to the door handle, turning it and pushing gently

It opened with a faint squeak.

Smith was where the figure had left him, a huge puddle of water around the base of the chair where his body had voided on death. Alvarez put her gun away and took her phone out, calling the emergency teams.

Alvarez read through the notes that Smith had made, some of it was wild speculation, some of it well reasoned, some of it was clearly caffeine induced madness. Alvarez leaned back in her chair, looking down at her desk and the figurine sat there.

It was a sure bet that having that was what had got Smith killed…

Alvarez went back to the report, Smiths neat handwriting constant throughout. Theories on the figurine, on the believers of Ran and how such a figurine would be holy to the point that only their priests would be allowed to touch it. On the last page, something else, same pen, different writing, looking like someone had scribbled it with clumsy hands.

Give. It. Back.

Smith had been found with a pen underneath his chair, he'd managed to work one of his hands free before he'd died, were these his last words?

“What if it was all about this?” Alvarez leaned flat on the desk, looking at the figurine and then up at Richards, “What if the killer is fixated on this and all they’re after is this?”

“They could have taken it with them at any time,” Richards said, “It was right there, every time, why wouldn’t they just take it and be done?”

“Maybe part of their narrative is that they can’t just take it?” Alvarez said, “What if they need someone to give it to them?”

“Batshit crazy is batshit crazy,” Richards replied, “But if they’re coming after this, we can use that to bait a trap for them.”

“Means putting out one of our own for this psycho to come after, I’m not happy with it.”

“I’m up for it Boss; they need to be brought down, no one takes one of our own and gets away with it. I’ll take it, my place is far more secure than Smiths and we can have units ready to roll when the nutter turns up.

They only got away with Smith because he lived in a shit apartment block with no cameras, surrounded by scrotes who wouldn't raise a finger to save anything but their own benefits..."

"I don't think we'll get approval, but I'll run it up the chain."

Two days later, Alvarez watched all the cameras set up in Richards' place as he moved around, the tension in his movements giving away his fear. There were more than twenty officers in the area, some in local bars, some in houses nearby, some on the streets and in cars, no way was anything getting close to Richards without them knowing. Alvarez looked around the street, late in the evening now, the darkness was all pervading, and Richards had just gone to the toilet.

The one place that he'd insisted there were no cameras...

Alvarez waited, glancing at her watch as five minutes passed by, ten. She tried to remember if he'd taken his phone in with him, was he in trouble or just doomscrolling like most men do?

Twenty minutes…

Twenty five…

“All units,” Alvarez spoke into her radio, “Anything, Anywhere?”

Nothing

Alvarez looked around the street again, then high, across the rooftops.

Getting silly now, no one’s going to be…

There were missing roof tiles three houses down, enough that a person could climb through the hole. Houses of that time usually had linked roof space, separated only by thin brick or plaster walls…

“Unit one, make a walk by,” Alvarez spoke into the radio.

On the street, Daniels came around the corner and went up to Richards' front door, knocking with reasonable force. It wasn't the first time that Daniels had been around the house, they often played poker there together.

The killer shouldn't suspect

Daniels knocked again, harder this time. "OI, RICHARDS, DON'T BE LEAVING ME OUT HERE IN THE COLD..."

No response

"Ma'am," Daniels voice was urgent over the radio, "No response and I can hear water running in the upstairs bathroom."

"Breach," Alvarez replied instantly, "All units converge..."

Daniels kicked the door in, special operations swarming in from the nearby van. Shouting from inside the house and a single gunshot.

Richards had been on the toilet…

The tattoo was still fresh and he's been tied to the toilet using the belt from his trousers and the sash from his bathing robe, obvious lacerations around the mouth where the shower cord had been forced into his mouth, but as the medics worked, shuddering gouts of water erupted from his throat.

“Is he alright?” Alvarez asked.

“No,” The Paramedic said, still working, “He's swallowed more water than anyone should have done, we need to get him to hospital before he has an edema.”

“Go, Go…” Alvarez turned to the special operations captain. “Did you get the bastard alive?”

“We got them.” The captain looked grim, “Is this the one you've been working on for a few years now?”

“I hope so,” Alvarez said.

The young woman restrained on the bed didn't seem like she'd have presented much of a threat to trained officers like Smith and Richards, but as she looked around the room, Alvarez was reminded that the most dangerous creature are often the smallest, as their venom was more concentrated.

And this one had plenty of venom…

The woman's eyes came to rest on Alvarez, no trace of empathy, no hint of concern for her own fate or anyone else's.

"DI Alvarez," Alvarez said by way of introduction, "and you are?"

"But a humble servant of the goddess," The woman said, "We who are bound to service have no need of names, that the goddess knows us is enough."

One of those then…

“Can you tell me why?” Alvarez asked, “Why the killings, for what reason?”

“You saw the notes from your fellow officer,” The woman kept her eyes on Alvarez, “You could have ended this by handing back the effigy, no one else had to die.”

“You could have just taken it,” Alvarez said, “Any of the times that you killed someone, you could have just taken it.”

“I am forbidden from touching it, the punishment for handling it is death, those are the laws of the goddess…”

“So, anyone who’s touched the figurine has to die?” Alvarez asked.

“Those are the laws,” The woman held Alvarez’s gaze evenly. “That’s why your friends had to die.”

“Richards didn’t die,” Alvarez replied.

"Did he not…?" The woman's tone bore no hostility, only the certainty of purpose. "I think you should check again."

Alvarez took her phone out and dialled the other hospital, "How's Richards doing?"

There was a pause on the line and the sound of the phone being passed over, "This is DI Lomax, I'm sorry Alvarez, we didn't want to interrupt your questioning."

"Is he alright?"

"I…" A pause, the faintest sigh, "No, Richards is gone, the two officers watching him waited till everyone was gone and then finished the job that your suspect started."

"*Our people* killed him?"

"Looks that way," Lomax said, "Watch yourself over there."

Alvarez hung up and looked at the woman, "How…?"

The woman said nothing.

Alvarez felt a spike of anger rising up her back and marched from the room, heading back to the station and returning an hour later. Alvarez walked back into the woman's room, her bag over her shoulder.

"How many of you are there?" Alvarez asked.

The woman said nothing.

Alvarez reached into the bag and took out the figurine, the woman's mouth dropping open in shock, "You *dare* to touch the holy…"

"Not just me," Alvarez stepped in and put the figurine on the woman's hand.

"No, NO," The woman struggled to sit up, looking down in terror, "I'm forbidden to touch it."

“If you don’t help me now, we’re both dead,” Alvarez said, “talk, how do we stop this?”

“You can’t,” The woman lay back in the bed. “Don’t you see it’s the will of the goddess.”

“Then who do we give it back to?” Alvarez leaned closer, taking the figurine back, “Or this goes on forever, this gets discarded, sent to charity, someone else picks it up and dies, do you want to see more death? Is that what this is really about?”

The woman stared up at Alvarez and then leaned back, “The Sea,” she said, “When it goes back to the sea, the goddess will be appeased.”

“That’s it?” Alvarez looked at her in disbelief, “All someone had to do was throw this in the water and it’s all over? None of you could have done that?”

“Not without dying ourselves. None of us wanted to die, we are only to carry out the will of the Goddess. Do you not understand faith and belief, detective?”

“I’m glad I don’t,” Alvarez put the figurine back in her bag, “I’ll leave a guard on the door.”

“Why?” The woman smiled, “I accept my fate, I will take the water gladly, and when you feel it, so will you…”

“We’ll see…”

Alvarez left the hospital, heading down to her car and out to the east coast, aware that another car was following her at every twist and turn of the road. She drove down to the sea front and stepped out into the faint drizzle. She took the figurine out, turning to see the figures getting out of the car that had followed her, all of them dressed in long green robes, none of them moving towards her.

“This is what it’s all about?” Alvarez called to them.

They said nothing.

Alvarez turned and hurled the figurine as hard as she could, it soared over the edge of the dock and splashed into the water below. She turned back, fully expecting to have to fight off the figures in the green robes.

They were leaving.

Three were already in the car, the last one pausing at the rear door, raising their hand as if in farewell before stepping in. The car backed out of the parking lot and drove away, leaving Alvarez wet and cold on the docks. She got back in her car and drove back, some part of her fully expecting the woman to be already dead, but when she arrived, she found the woman sat up in bed, a nurse checking her vitals.

“You did it,” The woman said, breaking into a broad smile, “Oh thank the goddess it’s over.”

“It’s not over,” Alvarez said, “You still have to pay for what you did, and we’re going to find your friends too.”

“*Find* them?” The woman looked bemused.

Alvarez glanced sideways as the lift chimed and an orderly pushed an empty bed out, heading for a different ward. “We *will* find them, and you’ll all pay for what you did.”

“Oh Detective…” The woman leaned back in the bed, pulling up her hospital gown to reveal the tattoo over her stomach, “I’m happy to pay for what you did to me.”

Alvarez felt a sense of rising fear as she looked around the bed, seeing the two sealed fifteen litre water cooler bottles by the side of the bed.

“One for me,” The woman said, “One for you.”

The Nurse reached down for the first bottle and placed it on the bedside table, taking the seal off as the woman laid back.

“Whoa,” Alvarez felt a chill of fear as she realised that the nurse was one of the cult. “Put that down,” She reached for her radio.

“That won’t help, Detective,” The woman looked at her, “Don’t worry, here comes *your* bed.”

Alvarez jumped as she heard a blast of air to the side of her, reaching up to pick the dart out of her neck, the orderlies strong hands catching her as she felt her legs buckle. She laid on the bed as it was wheeled into the room and placed next to the woman. No longer able to co-ordinate her movements, she felt the woman's hand on hers.

"Don't worry, we'll soon be with the goddess..." The woman laid back and tilted her head back as the nurse placed the water bottle in her mouth, holding it upright so that the water poured in. The sound of gulping and gasping for air filled the room as the woman began to drink the whole bottle, the nurse reciting something in a guttural dialect.

Alvarez felt consciousness slipping as she felt the orderly laying her flat on the bed, looking through lidded eyes as a second nurse came into the room, fitting a long hose to the end of the other water bottle.

"You don't have to worry, Detective," The woman said, "We know you can't meet the goddess like our sister is doing, so we'll make it easy for you, like your colleagues..."

The faint sound of buzzing came from the other side of the bed as the orderly turned back with a tattoo gun in his hand, a faint pain in her neck as he started the cover work.

Alvarez head was tipped back and she closed her eyes, surrendering to the darkness…

At least it ends here.

The three people stood looking at the two bodies, the empty bottles on the bedside.

“It’s over?” The man dressed as an orderly asked.

“Our sisters sacrifice will give us time to regroup,” The woman who had administered the water to Alvarez reached into her pockets and pulled out a small green figurine identical to the one that had been thrown in the sea. “But the work has not finished, not by a long way.”

The other nurse and the orderly made a brief bow to her, speaking in unison.

"Yes, High Priestess..."

Follow John and his work here:

ADRIENNE

BY
GENE BAKER

Serial Killers

The first time I dreamed of Adrienne was within days after leaving the hospital where I had been since, what I was told, had been an accidental contact with an exposed high-voltage cable that nearly killed me. It occurred the night before my fourteenth birthday. For several weeks after that, the girl who appeared to be the same age as me with shoulder-length brunette hair and startling gray eyes would occasionally join me in my slumbers.

The dreams, though short and infrequent, were extremely vivid. For instance, we danced (if you can call it that) on the back porch at my house to a Beatles song playing on what appeared to be a small, battery powered, AM radio. Another time, I was with her as she seemed to luxuriate in not only the sunshine but the absolute joy of watching everyone enjoying it as well at the public swimming pool in Chapman Park.

Beautiful and sweet were those nighttime escapes. In terrible contrast to my real-life world of bullying at school and alcohol-fueled mental and physical abuse at home. At sixteen, I committed the moral equivalent of suicide by running away.

That was when I met the man known as “Father Rick”. A Catholic priest whose full name was

Ricardo Martinez. I immediately assumed that it was the first time we had come into contact with each other but something kept nagging at me about a sense of familiarity.

His calling was to work “The Underground” among the indigent and runaways like me. He had noticed me as he made his rounds and approached me with the only kind hand I had encountered in a long while. Being angry with the world and distrusting of everyone in it, I rejected his offer and slipped back into my cold-hearted life among the shadows of Houston’s skyscrapers.

The next time I crossed paths with Father Martinez was in a courtroom. He had convinced the Judge to give me a choice; go to prison for Grand Theft and Failure to Register for the Draft or into the military. Being that the war in Vietnam was still going strong the Army wasn’t too picky about whom they would take in to be “Cannon Fodder”.

A little over two years later, I found myself bleeding out on the deck of a River Patrol Boat in the middle of the Mekong Delta. By then, Adrienne had become a nearly forgotten and ethereal childhood memory.

Serial Killers

Houston Police Detective Paul Graham had just pulled the bedsheet back over the face of the disfigured murder victim in front of him when Officer Parker yelled to him from the hallway, “Hey Lieutenant! That priest you called in is here!”.

“About damn time! Send ‘I’m in.” Graham huffed, showing his anger over the crime scene before him. “*What kind of sick bastard would do this?*” He silently asked himself.

“Sorry about taking so long to get here.” Father Martinez apologized, “It was bumper-to-bumper on the Six-Ten.”

As Graham reached over to pull back the sheet from the teenage girl’s corpse he groused, “Better late than never, I guess.”

Suddenly, the cleric put his hand out to stop the reveal. Slightly startled by the move, the Detective defensively said, “I didn’t think you would be so squeamish about this sort of thing. Devil worship and rituals being your forte and all.”

"Squeamishness has nothing to do with it, Paul. That flowery scent that hit me the second I stepped into the room pretty much tells me what I need to know."

"Really! Do you mind filling me in?"

The Priest looks quickly around the girl's bedroom and his concentration falls on the cracked mirror over the vanity before answering, "I conjecture that the eyes were burned out of her head as if with a blowtorch and no other obvious injuries. There's also no evidence of forced entry."

Wide-eyed with surprise, Graham asks, "And what about that perfume? We figured that it was poured over her as part of some ceremony."

"That is not perfume, and there was no ritual here. It is a Sign."

"A sign of what?"

"I've only heard second-hand about this kind of thing. For the last several months, on the night of the full moon, just like last night, there has been a killing like this."

"I haven't heard about that." Graham says with a sideways glance of annoyance.

"You wouldn't. What happens among those poor souls in The Underground, stays in The Underground. Besides, the alligators and swift undercurrents down there in the channel usually take care of what's left. You guys only get involved when some young white girl living in a wealthy neighborhood like Pine Terrace gets murdered."

"I'll try not to be too insulted by what you just said." The Police Lieutenant growled. "Is there anything you Can do with us now?"

Grinning with self-satisfaction at the response that his snarky jab elicited, Martinez replied with more sincerity, "I'll put in a call to the Bishopric in New Orleans to confirm if my suspicions are true."

"And if you find out that your 'Suspicions are true'?"

Shaking his head slowly, the priest says in a quiet tone, “In that case this…Is the kind of evil that neither of us, in all of our past experiences, is adequately prepared to deal with.”

Lieutenant Graham stood up from behind his desk and waved his friend into his office. “Hey, Padre! You’re just in time for once.”

While pointing his open left hand at a tall woman in her mid to late thirties, he introduced, “Father Ricardo Martinez, this is Mrs. Lillian Wells and this is her son, Frank. This young man says he has some information about our case that he’d like to share. It seems our victim, Janie Whedbee, was his girlfriend. Is that right?”

“She liked to think so.” Was the teen boy’s mumbled reply.

The Detective sat down at his desk and began writing in his notebook. “When was the last time you had contact with her?”

“About a week ago, at the pool in Chapman Park.”

"Anything out of the ordinary happen there?"

Lifting the focus of his eyes from the top of his shoes to the scritching of the policeman's pencil on notepaper, Frank Wells speaks in little more than a whisper, "She got into a fight with that new girl from Louisiana."

"What was the fight about?"

"Me."

Graham grinned broadly as he asked, "What about you?"

"Janie got mad because I was looking at Adrienne. Janie started yelling at her to stop flirting with me."

"You have a last name for this Adrienne?"

The boy shook his head slowly before admitting, "I can't pronounce it."

"How about Thivierge?" Martinez interjected.

After everyone in the room turned to look at the Priest, Wells said, “Yeah…That sounds about right.”

“I’ll talk to you in a minute, Father!” Graham snapped after an uncomfortable moment of silence. Then turning his questions back to the teenager in front of him, “Was it just an argument, or did it get physical.”

“Janie went to slap Adrienne but her boyfriend jumped up and took the lick.”

“Boyfriend’s name?”

“Jeremy MacAllen.”

“After that?”

“When Adrienne started growling, I got between them and ended it.”

“She Growled?” Graham asked incredulously.

Frank Wells tilted his head upward so that he was answering with utmost sincerity straight into the dubious eyes of his interrogator, “Yeah, like an angry dog.”

After closing the door behind Mrs. Wells and her son, the Detective turned his attention back to the priest that had remained behind. “Is that a Papal Seal I see there?” He asked while referring to the packet in Martinez’s lap.

“Yes, it is.” Was the solemn response. “It arrived by special courier this morning.”

“It looks pretty thick. Can you just give me the ‘Reader’s Digest’ version?”

“I’ll see what I can do but, I’m telling you from the very beginning, Detective Graham, if I am right about this, the four corners of the earth are littered with the remains of others who investigated this same situation.”

“That sounds ominous!”

After a doubt-filled moment of hesitation, Father Rick says sullenly, “Okay. All this started around three hundred years ago. Adrienne Marie Thivierge was born in the Year of Our Lord in 1650. When she was ten, her father, Louis Thivierge, was appointed by the King of France to be the Tax Collector to the trade settlement on Isle Dauphin. What is today, the island of Madagascar.

“Things went okay for a while until a disease, thought to be Typhus, hit the island and killed Louis and his two sons. When their only girl began showing symptoms, her mother, Béatrice, couldn't stand the thought of losing her entire family. Since European and Church-sanctioned Medicine didn’t do any good, she compromised her faith and took Adrienne to a native healer.”

Looking up from the file in his lap to try and emphasize what Graham was to be told next, Martinez saw the policeman had his head cocked slightly to the side and staring blankly at him. “Am I boring you, Detective?”

“Not at all! I’m just wondering how far afield you’re going with this.”

In exasperation, Father Rick took a deep breath and let it out slowly before saying, “I know this will be hard for you to believe. You really need to set your preconceived ideas aside for just the time being.”

“Sure. Go ahead.”

After a few seconds to put his thoughts back together, the dissertation continued. “The Healer, who had no love for the foreign invaders, tricked Béatrice. The girl was turned into a Vampire. But not the blood-drinking, ‘Dracula’ type that we are most familiar with. Adrienne became an ‘Astral Vampire’. One who feeds on human souls rather than blood. Béatrice was implanted with a hell-borne parasite.

“Once a month, on the night of the full moon, an inhuman entity that resides in Adrienne leaves her body, while she is in a trance, and goes out to feed. The entity uses any reflective object nearby, like that mirror in Janie’s bedroom, to transport itself into the presence of its next victim. It is also connected with Adrienne by a Metaphysical Umbilical Cord called a ‘Silver Rope’.

“As you may have heard, ‘The eyes are the windows to the soul.’, That is how the thing acquires its spiritual food. The dark energy burns the eyes out as the soul leaves the victim.”

Graham inquires sullenly, “So, I guess we need something like a wooden stake to put an end to this?”

With an impatient tone to his voice, Martinez responded, “It’s not as easy as that. There are only two known ways of ending this. One is to sever the Silver Rope with what legend calls, ‘The Sword of The King’ which sends the entity straight back to Hell while keeping Adrienne still alive.

“Since no one knows what the Sword is or where it is located, that leaves us with the other, more gruesome, alternative. That is to decapitate the girl.”

Seeming to ignore the horrendous idea of beheading a child, Graham asks, “That is if we can get past Béatrice, right?”

Temporarily stunned by his friends' seeming lack of empathy for Adrienne, it took a few seconds before Martinez could get his mind back on track. “Béatrice is ten times stronger, faster, and more agile than any normal human but, the real danger is the thing that is possessing Adrienne. If it feels its existence in this world is threatened, it can summon a horde from Hell itself in defence. Our only hope of success is to catch it in the daytime when, while it is still powerful, it is at its weakest.”

“Do you have any cavalry that can be called in if necessary?”

“Sounds like you are starting to believe in this!”

“All the freakish things we’ve experienced in the past would keep me from rejecting this whole thing outright. Or until someone comes up with a more believable story, I’ll go with it.”

“I do have one other resource I can tap into. I’ll contact her this afternoon and get back to you. Are you going to question the MacAllen boy?”

“Yup!”

The first single-story, ranch-style home in the Garden Heights area of Houston, was built in nineteen-fifty-three. The proud and well-kept homes would become a memorial to the fleeting prosperity of "Baby Boom" America.

In general, people in this subdivision and others like it were "Neighbors". They gathered every so often for holiday barbecues, and some school functions, and generally looked out for one another. However, behind the perfectly manicured lawns and meticulously maintained facades, cruel and painful secrets were often hidden.

Every street had at least one person who would be known as the "Neighborhood Snoop". Little that happened in the public areas surrounding the homes went unnoticed and Mrs. Landsteiner was one such individual.

As soon as Detective Graham pulled up and parked his car in front of the MacAllen house he saw Landsteiner come quickly out of her own home and start watering the lawn. She would drench the same area of grass the whole time she stood staring across the street. He made a mental note to talk to the woman after he finished with the boy.

With no answer to his repeated phone calls, he decided to check out the residence in person. As Graham was leaving the station that morning, a Children's Services Officer, Sargeant Leticia Cabrera, approached him. "I hear that you are going to talk to a certain Jeremy Todd MacAllen." She said in her usual quiet, almost whispering voice.

"Yup. You know something about him?" Replied the Detective.

As she handed over a file with the subject's name on it, Cabrera explained, "Back in April, Jeremy decided he had had enough and fought back against one of the kids that were bullying him named Mark Stevens. Put Stevens in a coma for three days."

"What the Hell?" Graham exclaimed as he looked at the kids' file photo. Short, slim, with a crew cut of red hair and a face full of freckles, the boy looked the part of a schoolyard target.

"A pound-and-a-half rock up the side of your head will do that."

“Any mention of a girl named Adrienne Thivierge?”

“You mean his ‘Girlfriend’?” Leticia replied as she made the quotation marks in the air with her hands.

“Yeah.”

“She is a new student at Waller Junior High who arrived from New Orleans back in January. She has since become close to Jeremy.”

Graham was halfway up the driveway when his thoughts were interrupted by hearing Landsteiner shout, “Ain’t nobody there!

The boy left early this morning, and the parents are at work!”

“Thank You!” He shouted back as he opened his coat to reveal his badge. “I’ll just leave my card then!”

“Bonjour Père!” Doctor Gabrielle Boudreau said with a slight Creole accent as she gently grasped Father Martinez’s hand. “It has been way too long for us.”

"It was that mission trip to Haiti two years ago, I believe."

"Yes, I believe it was! So, what brings you here? Going back to Haiti?"

"Not this time Gabbie. I have to pick your brain."

The thin black woman with streaks of prematurely gray hair smiles broadly and asks her friend, "Oh my! What about?"

Rick moved in close to speak in a conspiratorial whisper. "Adrienne Thivierge."

The Medical Doctor took two steps back and turned ashen as she asked, "She is here?"

"Yes."

"Oh My! May the Good Lord grant you mercy and protection! You are not going after her, are you?"

"A friend of mine with the HPD is and I feel that he needs help on it."

Looking around her to see if anyone else in the small, rundown clinic was listening, Boudreau took Father Rick by his elbow and led him into her office. After quietly closing the door, she turns around and gruffly asks, "Have you lost your mind? This is some serious dread we're talking about!"

"I know. But I was hoping there would be some advantage that you could give us."

With her hands on her hips, Gabrielle Boudreau declares with an all-knowing scowl, "You mean Voudon!"

"Yes." Martinez replied almost sheepishly.

"You boys have no idea of the pile of shit you have decided to step into!"

Martinez knew from experience that it did no good to bring up Gabbie's frequent use of expletives, so he let it slide, again.

Boudreau asks nervously, “I can’t talk you out of this?”

“I’m afraid not.” Was the timid reply.

Adrienne’s next door neighbors, Mike and Teresa Bledsoe, had welcomed and befriended the girl and her mother. Within earshot of Jeremy, they had mentioned how much they loved and missed the Crawfish Etouffee from when they lived in New Orleans. Teresa had gotten the recipe for the dish from a friend and looked forward to the opportunity to try it. Upon hearing that, Jeremy immediately told them that he knew where to get the crustaceans in abundance and had come with Adrienne to the local swamp known as “Turkey Bayou”. He hoped that his skills as a “Provider” would impress Adrienne, and he was right.

The girl would exclaim with delight, “Oh my! How wonderful!” Every time Jeremy pulled up a coffee can trap loaded down with the delicacy. However, as they began the long walk back to the Bledsoe house, a heavy sadness overtook her.

No longer able to withhold the question that gnawed at him, Jeremy sat down on a park bench and patted the empty seat beside him. Taking the indicated action, Adrienne slowly sat down next to her friend. “Okay.” MacAllen quietly said before asking, “What’s wrong?”

“I don’t want this to end.” The girl replied so softly that it could barely be heard.

When tears began to slowly roll down Adrienne’s cheeks. He carefully reached out and hesitantly placed his hand on top of hers.

She choked as the words left her mouth. “I have to leave this place. Probably forever.”

Jeremy felt as if he had been punched hard in the gut such that he was barely able to croak out, “Why?”

The girl looks up as her eyes, streaked with red, lock onto the second-story bedroom of the house across the street. The Whedbee house. “Because of what happened to Janie.”

"Whattaya mean? You didn't have anything to do with that!"

Turning back to look the saddened boy in the eyes, a gentle expression of compassion moves across Adrienne's face. Then, leaning forward, she asks with a sob stuck in her throat, "Would you kiss me goodbye?" As she closes her eyes and slightly puckers her mouth.

Jeremy MacAllen said nothing. He moved in close and emptied his entire being into the warm, soft lips that responded by gently caressing his own.

Suddenly Jeremy's brain seemed to explode in an onslaught of nightmarish images. When he was finally able to open his eyes and recover his senses, it was the near dark of evening. He found it hard to breathe because of the painful pounding in his chest. The sun had just descended below the horizon and Adrienne and the burlap sack of "Mud Bugs" were gone.

Doctor Boudreau had held herself back from the assault on the abomination's lair, but not because of fear. She had a "Sense" that her purpose here was in a different direction she couldn't, for the time being, know.

A woman's piteous scream emanates from somewhere in the large house and she feels her startled heart slam against her back. Within seconds Gabrielle also hears what she can only assume is Lieutenant Graham smashing through the double front door of the old mansion. "There goes the element of surprise!" She says to herself.

A movement out of the corner of her eye causes the Doctor to turn her head to get a better look and she notices a male teenager sneaking up the cement sides of the open storm drain behind the nearly century-old manor. As the boy grunts hard and lifts a broken piece of concrete over a sunken section of ground, he is startled to hear a woman with a deep accent angrily ask, "Just what do you think you are doing here?"

Jeremy MacAllen quickly reacts by dropping the slab while simultaneously drawing a large hunting knife from its sheath.

“Don’t try to stop me!” He snarled at the woman, “Adrienne needs me. They are going to kill her, and I won’t let that happen!”

Gabrielle motions for him to hush himself. “Are you that girl’s boyfriend? Is she calling you? In your head I mean.”

“I haven’t got time for this!”

“Sure. I don’t know why I didn’t think of this before. You love her don’t you?”

“Is it that obvious?”

“Yes, it is. I will go with you. I will help you.”

The maze of tunnels and rooms Boudreau and MacAllen find themselves navigating was built in 1908 by the home’s original owners. Dire predictions about the coming of Halley’s Comet in 1909, sent many wealthy people to construct underground “Shelters” to wait out the apocalypse. Now it served as an easily secured hideaway for Adrienne and Béatrice.

Because it was built in haste, some of the latter areas had fallen in over the years. This created a dark, cobweb-strewn, and confusing dust-filled obstacle course that only the bearings Adrienne was mentally sending to her love allowed them to get through. The pair paused and squeezed

themselves into a small nook when the sounds of the terrible battle ahead of them abruptly ceased.

Peering out through a broken section of a wall, Gabrielle sees a woman in the dim light that she assumes is Béatrice facing away from her. The back of the filthy shirt she is wearing is riddled with the ragged, funnel-shaped holes made by large calibre bullets having gone completely through, front to back. A thick, black fluid that can only be conjectured as being what accounts for blood in the “Zombie”, oozes from the rapidly closing wounds. The policeman’s .357 Magnum pistol had, apparently, done little more than further anger the monster.

Gabbie whispered to Jeremy, "Give me that knife of yours." As he hesitantly hands it over to her, she takes it, wraps her Rosary around it, and silently prays, "*Dear God, guide my hand so that this instrument of your power is true to your will.*"

Turning to Jeremy she points to her right and again whispers, "Go on ahead. Now!"

Hearing the boy running down the passageway behind her, Béatrice turns away from Paul Graham's torn and broken body which is lying next to the similarly brutalized Bledsoe's. In an instant, the knife flew through the air and crunched through the skull at her right temple. The creature staggered as it tried to stay on its feet before falling backward in a heap to the floor.

Gabrielle walked up to the quickly decomposing corpse and started to untie a raw silk bag. As she is doing this, there was the sound of cracking bones as Béatrice's face split open and a large, black, slug-like thing sprouts spindly legs and began to crawl out of its suddenly non-functioning host.

Gabbie threw a portion of the contents from the gris-gris bag onto the unnatural horror causing it to burst into flames. “That’s all for you, you evil bitch!” She hissed.

As Jeremy ran into the main subterranean room, he sees a bruised and bleeding Father Martinez being held down on his back, helpless, by a hideous semblance of Adrienne. The demon opens its overly elongated and fanged maw and the priest’s eyes start bulging as if they would burst. Looking over at the ornate bed in the corner with a thick down mattress and pillows, Jeremy sees Adrienne lying there with her eyes closed as if she was asleep. He runs over to her, grabs her by the shoulders, and shakes her while shouting in desperation, “Adrienne! Wake up!”

All around him, a brilliant white light flashes amid the ear-splitting sound of thousands of tormented souls screaming.

For a moment, he looks down to see Adrienne looking up at him and smiling before his consciousness is swallowed by an infinite darkness.

Serial Killers

After recuperating at the Naval Hospital in San Diego for several painful months, I was medically discharged and took a plane back home to Houston.

That was when I went to meet with Father Rick at his new parish since he no longer worked the streets of The Underground. I thought I would feel my ribs crack as he enthusiastically embraced me with genuine gladness at my presence.

After briefly catching up on past events, I decided it was time to abruptly change conversational direction and asked, “What happened to Adrienne?”

With Father Martinez, looking like a deer on a nighttime country road stunned by the sudden appearance of headlights, I decided to bring him up to speed. “I guess you could say that my second Near Death Experience in Vietnam allowed me to recall events that were wiped out by the first one when I was a kid. I came to the realization that those “Dreams” of Adrienne proved to be, in actuality, bits of memory.”

I then reached into my shirt pocket and pulled out a carefully folded strip of black-and-white photos of the kind taken four for a dollar in booths at the County Fair and handed them over. “I salvaged these and some other of my stuff from the garbage pile that the new owners of my parent’s house had set out by the curb.

“It was then that I remembered how disappointed I was with the record of my first ‘Unofficial’ date with Adrienne because her image was so fuzzy. Like she wasn’t completely there. Now I know why.”

Slowly recovering his composure the priest responded, “Well, I guess it is time that you knew the truth.” Taking a moment to inhale a deep breath before letting it heavily out he continues, “Adrienne survived. Before she was possessed, she was dying of Typhus. It was a death sentence in the seventeenth century, but not today. It’s a good thing Doctor Boudreau was there. She did chest compressions on you to bring you back. Then, she led Adrienne’s treatment that saved her life as well.”

“That is great! But what happened to that…Thing?”

“Right back in Hell where it belongs thanks to you.”

After the extended pause elicited by that statement, the Father continued, “Gabbie is the one that figured this out. One of the ways to separate Adrienne from the entity that possessed her was with the mythical ‘Sword of The King’. ‘The King’ in this case refers to God. In scripture, for example, 1 John 4:16 says, “God is love.” Therefore, it is the most potent weapon in the arsenal against the forces of Satan. You loved Adrienne, and when you went to try and wake her up, you inadvertently severed the ‘Umbilical Cord’ that kept them joined. Therefore you, my friend, are the weapon that freed her. Unfortunately, exposure to that much dark power was, for you, like being struck by lightning. Thus, your long-term amnesia of those events from around that time.”

With barely constrained excitement at the thought of a reunion, I couldn’t help but ask, “So where is Adrienne now? Can I see her?”

“She was set up with a special foster family in New Orleans after spending a lot of time in rehabilitation. After all, she had over three hundred years of trauma to struggle through. But she did well, even though she thinks you are dead.”

“What? Whatta ya mean, ‘Dead’?”

With a look of worried suspicion, the priest’s tone changed slightly, “That brings us to the answer to your second question. It was thought best at the time for her treatment, but I didn’t agree with it. I was overruled by none other than the Holy Father himself.”

I sank heavily back into my chair not knowing what to do with this information when Father Rick bent his head slightly as if in prayer, “I suppose one could say that your coming here today was a most providential event after all, Jeremy.”

“How’s that?” I harrumphed back.

“You see, I have been asked to officiate this weekend. At Adrienne’s wedding.”

I saw that Martinez could sense the none-too-subtle mixture of anger and disappointment that crushed the hopes of the man in front of him. Then he said in that “Teaching Moment” voice of his, “You were thirteen, Jeremy. Surely you didn’t think that…”

"You don't understand, Padre." I interrupted. "I saw Everything the day I kissed her on that bench. I literally stepped into Hell itself! I was only pulled back by the love that Adrienne and I had for each other. I just find it hard to believe that much has changed. There's gotta be a reason that I have suddenly remembered it all! I mean, after all this time, and her so-called 'Treatment' what could be the harm in it?"

After a wrenching, long silence, I looked up to see a sly grin slowly spread across the Priest's face as one was forming on my own. "Better late than never." He almost whispered.

"You ready for a Road Trip, Father?"

"I don't know how Adrienne and her Foster Parents will react to you pulling this 'Lazarus Thing' on them."

"I guess we'll just have to find out!"

So now Father Rick and I are headed to New Orleans pushing this old Buick as hard and as fast as it will go.

Follow Gene and his work here:

Serial Killers

HAND DELIVERED

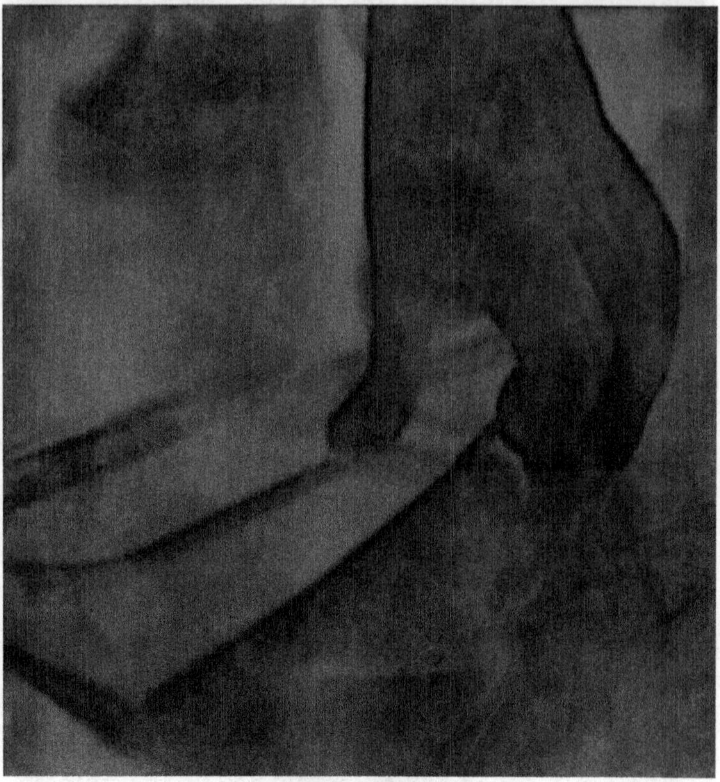

BY
M PURKISS

Serial Killers

I know what you're going to think. You'll think I'm sick, that I should be locked up. That the things I do for fun and thrill are far from normal. But, who's to say what's normal. I'm just as normal as you are. I have the same urges, the same feelings. The difference is that I'm brave enough to pursue my passion and follow what my heart wants, even when this comes with ending the lives of people. You may call them innocent, but I don't think that's valid, everybody had skeletons, everyone had flaws. I admit that sometimes I feel a twinge of something within me, that maybe I had gone too far, but then how far is too far. Sometimes, I think I might be slightly unhinged, but there are many others out there like me, there are people who can appreciate my art. The number of bodies I've used for my entertainment and scored off my checklist has increased significantly lately, and I love changing the ways I express myself. The way it all ends. I am always amazed with the creativity I show when I get a new, let's say, project to work on.

Starting out, it was just something to try, something to dabble in. It was never meant to turn out as big as it is now, but then my obsessive nature wouldn't let me slow down. It wouldn't let me stop, it became my life, but I learned to value my work. I gained satisfaction from every new notch I made in my belt. I'm not a violent person, I'm actually shy and timid, but they say its always the quiet ones you need to watch out for. I just found a way to get my frustrations out and I discovered I was good at it. I am an expert with my instruments, an artist, a creative. The lengths I have gone to before now has achieved some exciting situations. I recall a time when I had managed to catch someone in broad daylight, maybe you saw it on the news. She was a lovely girl; I just walked up and propelled my sharpened blade into her back and carried on walking as the blood drained from her body. But I digress, I try not to do the same thing twice, variety is of course the spice of life.

Never before have I sent anything like this to one of my recipients, but there is something special I feel inside about you. There is something about you which makes me want to just spill my guts, figuratively speaking. I feel comfortable. Well, of course, I've known about you for a while, even if it's not mutual. I feel like I've painted a perfectly clear picture in my mind about you. I know you on the outside, but I can't wait to know you on the inside. I wonder if your blood feels the same as the others, warm as it falls over my hands. You feel so different; I regularly sit here and wonder why, but as of yet am unable to get the answers I desperately seek. I know where you work, I know where you shop, I know where you eat. I even know the colour of your underwear. I have a keen eye, I'm like a ninja, you'll never see me if I don't want you to. I'm like a ghost, a spectre, a breeze in the air. I'm that shadow you get in the corner of your eye, when you have seen something, but it turns out that nothing is there. Or at least you don't think anything is there. That little feeling you get inside your head, that's me in case you're wondering.

Every time I smell your perfume I go wild inside. I really want to push my head on your bare skin and sniff, its intoxicating. Its magnificent the way it scents the air around you as you walk or fills the room as you enter. I found the exact one online, I sometimes spray it on my skin and pretend we've been in a passionate embrace.

After I end a life, I then have the problem of the corpse. What to do with it? I sometimes cut them up and grind them down into mince and throw it away with my food waste. Sometimes I use acid, but with that is the smell of the toxic fumes, something my asthma can't handle. Damn these human conditions. I have used animals before, but besides pigs there are not many that will eat the bones. So, I try and do what I can to get them out as quick as possible, because the smell of decomposing meat is quite overpowering. I used to cut the bodies up and put them in my freezer, until my freezer became full. I sometimes take the bodies on road trips, from place to place, and dispose of them in different counties. Doing this gives the police something “proper” to do, but I’m confident they will never connect the dots back to me. I do feel untouchable sometimes, but I can’t afford to be too cocky, so every now and then I have a reality check, a little reflection. I sit back and contemplate my next moves. I will normally get a burger and a thick vanilla milkshake, whilst trying not to make the flesh which has embedded itself under my nails obvious to the poor fast-food worker. When I’m sat there, sometimes I ponder what it would feel like to force their hand into a fryer and hold it there. Would the flesh bubble? Would the flesh fall off the bone like tender meat? My stomach is grumbling now as I write, thinking about it.

Knowing what I know now, I sometimes wonder if I would do anything differently. Probably not, but I can’t help the way my brain computes things. As soon as I get a moment by myself, my mind is going one hundred miles per hour, thinking of different scenarios and circumstances I could possibly form. Yes, I know, I’m sick, in your opinion. Maybe you’re sick, you haven’t stopped reading and I’m glad, there is still so much more I want to offload and let you know. I wish I was sat with you as you read my inner thoughts and feelings. I am very selective who I let into my life and for me to confide this with you is something I'm not used to. What you have done to me; the sensations you make me feel is unreal.

Its not all blood and guts with me don't get me misunderstood. When I'm not feeling like creating a masterpiece because of illness or lack of energy, I'm more than happy just to wrap my hands around someone's neck and watch as the life is drained from their eyes. At first, they always fight, but I always have the upper hand. Soon after, they realise it's a waste of time, submitting to what is happening. The pink tinged skin of their faces turn slightly blue until the life has gone, then it turns a slightly grey colour. I never lose eye contact; I like to watch that sparkle in their eyes disappear. I always take a big inhale as they take their last beath so I can feel their soul leave their body and pass through me. It's a surreal experience, five stars would highly recommend, but its not for everyone I'm well aware. Another benefit from creating this way is that there is minimal mess, nothing much to clean up. Well, just the useless mound of flesh, which is now dead weight, maybe that pun was intended, maybe not. Take it as you will.

Never before have I had such a fascination with someone as I do with you. I know eventually you'll probably end up the same as the others, but I have spent so much time observing you from near and far. I know you've felt me staring, I've noticed the feeling within when you've turned to look over your shoulder from the weight of my gaze. When you've been walking down the street, a cold shiver goes down your spine, like something is a bit strange. That's me watching your every contraction, watching your muscles move under the cover of skin, your joints move gracefully as you walk down the pathway, or even as you move to stand up from a chair. My limbs tingle at the thought of your activities, graceful, beautiful.

Thinking back to when I started, I promised myself that I would not become attached. That the people I pursue are separated completely. Emotionally and mentally. But as times gone on, I've found it interesting finding out about people's lives, observing them like a tourist on safari, watching their habits, what they do in their free time. Its interesting that everyone more or less does the exact same thing. They might have different jobs, different wages, different social habits. But at the bones of it, we are all creatures of habit. I find it funny. I have followed all sorts of people. Some had affairs, some had darker secrets who didn't realise I was watching their every move, some are sicker than you think I am. I'm always watching. I see all. As more time passed, I became more invested into the lives the people led, starting to make notes on them. Reems of paper, full of scribbles and notes, sheets I've used front and back. I started to become obsessed with my research. When it comes to you, I am the most invested I've ever been before. I am sat here looking at about five full notebooks of your information, plus all the extras, the loose papers I scribble on when I'm out and about. I have a few sketches as well, being a bit of an artist, it helps me to focus, gives me a visual aid. I was a bit annoyed this morning, because as I watched you leave your house my pen ran out, so I hadn't been able to document your activities in detail. I managed to remember most and quickly jotted it down as soon as I got the chance.

Of course, you are probably sat there in complete astonishment. Take a breath. No one would blame you if you felt a little hot under the collar, I understand to someone who hasn't freely vented themselves, it may come as a bit of a shock, reading some of the things I have mentioned so far. Well, that's if you are still reading, but then maybe it would be considered unwise to stop, just in case there is something within this passage to help towards salvation. There might be, I'm unsure myself at this stage. All I'm sure about, is that I want you to know me as well as possible. To understand what makes me tick, what motivates me, what urges me on. The answer to all three of those questions is simple. You.

You never know, in another life, you and I could have been really good friends. If you were more willing to express yourself, the way I do. I have a feeling inside of me that you think about it. Remember, I have seen you. I have seen the way you look at your boss and co-workers. I have seen the way you act when you are out with your so-called friends. I would watch them if I was you, they are not as innocent as you think. I have followed them too in the name of my research, I won't go into much detail, but let's just say they only keep you around to make themselves look good. I really don't want to ruin your illusion, but let's just say, the last time they cancelled on you, they still went out and had a good time. I suppose, in a way, it doesn't matter what I say, its not as if you can utter anything because of the way you have found out this information. It's a cruel life sometimes. Don't get me wrong, the majority of my life has been pretty good, there was a time when I had friends like yours and I saw through their disguise. That's when I took it upon myself to destroy them, to break my chains of social acceptance. The first, I battered with a sledgehammer in the face as he slept. The second, I threw an electrical appliance in the bath whilst she was washing away her sins. The third, I drained his oxygen tank so he couldn't have the rescue breaths he desperately needed, ending in asphyxiation. Of course, the police investigated but couldn't find anything due to my meticulous planning and execution. I'm full of double meanings and puns today, I'm on top form, it must be the excitement.

Obviously, there are always risks in the work I do. I need to really think about what I'm doing, how I'm doing it and the process of everything that happens after. Its almost as if I need to think of the end first and work backwards, just to ensure that everything is put in place and is ready to go. The exception of course is you, I know so much about you, but I haven't thought about my end goal. I keep starting to plan, but nothing seems to fit with your personality or character. I have a rope; I could make it look like suicide, but then where is the fun in that. I have guns, but then that's too quick. I have blades, but that is getting boring now. I'll have time to ponder that I suppose. I'll keep thinking. You'll know when I do.

Understanding what I do is difficult for people. I completely understand. We have been brainwashed to think and act in a certain way, anything outside of those perimeters is classed as strange and unusual. I'm one of the lucky ones that has managed to resist the brainwashing and managed to live outside of the boundaries. Its so freeing over here, I answer to no one. It's liberating.

Right or wrong, I will continue to carry out my work for as long as I'm able. As long as I'm enjoying myself, I don't see why I should stop. Unless, someone decides to stop me of course, which I think is unlikely considering the experience and preparation I put into everything.

Have you ever felt so sure about something, that you never stop to question it? That is how I feel when I am writing this to you. I know for definite this is what I am supposed to be doing. I feel that it is time to let someone know about my journey so far. Sometimes I feel like I've just begun, there are so many more things that I want to try and put into action. I just hope that I have enough time and life within me to complete my bucket list. Oh, how I wish you could see the things I've got planned.

Serial Killers

Obviously, when all is finished and I've mastered a piece of work, it is then up to the police to try and figure out what has happened, where the missing person has gone. At the beginning I used to hear police sirens going off and I would hold my breath, feeling only my heart pounding in my chest. Now though, I find excitement in the ride. Now when I hear the sirens, it takes me back to the latest project I had worked on and wonder how decomposed their bodies are, or how well digested the flesh is as it's being eaten by rodents.

Usually when I complete a job, I do take some time to reflect on what I have done. I make notes and lists of what went well and what could have gone better. It's a sort of appraisal with myself I suppose. I look at what my plans are for the coming months and how I have developed as time has gone on. I might be a bit bias, but I feel like my performance has grown considerably since I began my venture. I sit here and smile, knowing I need to write some things down in ways that you can understand, this being the job connotation. I have seen you in work, seen you complete hundreds of these performance review sheets, it is sort of what gave me the idea. Once I complete the paper to the best of my ability, I then file it alphabetically under the way I had assassinated the person. For example, S for suffocation or B for burning, I'm sure you get the notion. I used to file under the person's name, but I soon realised sometimes I didn't find time or have the interest to learn the name of the person, so this system turned out redundant.

Sleeping was something I used to find difficult. When I started, I would be awake for days and weeks at a time, thinking about everything. Had I left something at the scene? Had I picked the right option for disposal? So many questions. I found myself having to take strong sleeping meds to even have a chance, sometimes I had to dose myself to a comatose state just to get through. Don't mistake this as me having guilt or anything like that, I don't regret anything I have done. But remember, in those early days, I was still fighting through the barriers society had put up and until I broke through completely there were times when I would be staring up at the ceiling and worry that I had messed something up. I replayed the events in my head over and over like a movie on repeat.

Eventually, everything worked out in my head, it mostly does to be honest. I am blessed that I have my brain wired in a certain way that usually doesn't allow for much error. I remember growing up when I would bring home stray cats, dissecting them as they were trying to scratch at my skin. I attempted to keep them alive as long as possible, whilst at the same time, remove all the things within. It was like a real-life game of operation, which of course I was brilliant at. I never touch the sides and made the man's red nose light up, for one thing, I didn't like the noise it made. It made my insides stir, so at the threat of the sound, I always won.

After I have done what I need to do and file my papers away, it doesn't end there. I suppose in someways I can't completely change what I am, I am human unfortunately. I can remember everything I have done, and to whom I've done it too. It is always there within the filing cabinet of my mind.

Now might be a nice time to take a little break and think back about the things you have learned so far. I'm sure you still think that I'm sick, that I need locking up, but what is it going to achieve, really. You can't bring back those who I have taken. Plus, I wouldn't let a wall lined with steel bars stop me. I sometimes sit and plan what would happen if it did occur. Maybe I could make a little band of prisoners my allies. Maybe I could win over the guards, I am quite charismatic, it would be a walk in the park.

Do you ever think about your ending? Do you ever think of what the pain will be like? I think about this all the time. I am not scared of death, in fact it is the only thing that keeps me going, the promise one day it will all end. Most people like to think they will pass in their sleep, but how realistic is that. That must be the most boring way to die possible. Me, I want to die in the most spectacular way imaginable. Maybe they could bring back one of those old torture devices they used to use. Possibly the one where they saw you in half, letting the innards spill on the floor below. How amazing would that be, to die in such an unusual way by todays standards. I was always told to stand out.

With the way I have been observing you of late, I have noticed that you seem a little anxious going about your day-to-day life. At times I sit back and question what your so scared about. Life isn't that menacing, is it? Maybe you should take some advice from me. Don't worry what other people think, if you want to do something, you do it and feel proud for your achievements, the same way I do.

As I followed you to work the other day, I noticed and noted down that you have been taking a different route, there is no logical explanation for this, apart from you got bored of the normal way you went. It always happens eventually; people get bored and try and change things up. Trust me, I think you need to re-evaluate your life. The change of route will only suppress the boredom for a little while. You need big changes.

Take it from someone who has experienced more than most. Nothing good comes from being basic and tiresome. My notebooks on you are quite repetitive, which is another reason why I have taken it upon myself to reach out. As I said before, I feel so comfortable with you, to confide in you. But on the other hand, I would like you to have a slither of opportunity to make one final splash. Maybe now that you know your time is limited, it might give you a little push to be a little bit more daring.

Carving my life has been challenging, but I always get what I want, I don't let people who try and get me down win. When someone says that I can't do something, I will make sure that I do. I always go a step further and let them know that I have succeeded. For example, a few months ago, someone said I couldn't purchase petrol using the container that I had brought along with me. I ignored them of course, filling my chosen vessel, then paid for the petrol I had taken; I'm not a thief. Following the heated exchange that followed, I took it upon myself to follow the shop owner home, using the petrol I had bought to ignite a fire in his house. His body, now just ash amongst the rubble of the building he resided in.

Hopefully you're still there reading this. If you have made it this far into my ramblings then I applaud your dedication, maybe there is something I have missed within you, probably not, but maybe. See what you do to me; you make me question things more deeply than the others have. I'm sitting here looking at my phone, your face is both my home and lockscreen. I love just waking the device up and staring down at your smiling face. The pictures I got are from your social media pages, you are moderately active on them, enough for me to have a further in-depth look into your life.

Yesterday, after I knew you were settled in your work chair, I took a stroll along the river, it was peaceful. I listened to the birds and inhaled the sweet morning air. It made my body uplift, I felt positive. I felt like I was exactly where I was supposed to be. You must be confused about the seemingly random things I'm telling you. I know some of these accounts and confessions are disjointed and sometimes out of context, but that is how my brain works. I jump from one thing to another, I try and get down my thoughts and good ideas as quickly as I can, to ensure I don't forget them when the next load of information is dumped in my grey matter. My mind is always switched on, always ticking.

On one occasion a few weeks back, I made a point to meet you at your workplace. I wanted more than just to watch; I wanted an interaction. You probably don't even remember it. I held the door open for you. Can you remember? Most likely not, to the majority it would be an everyday thing, not important. That moment when you were so close, I felt a twinge in my palms, like they were ready to prey upon your perfect neck. I had to resist; I just wanted to hear your voice up close and personal. You said "thank you" to me, those words have been played on repeat in my skull ever since.

Understanding is key, which is why I want to reiterate why I'm telling you all this. It is a chance for you to get to know me, the same way I know you. I have told you some of my secrets and touched on my past. I haven't held back. I still know more about you than you do about me that's for sure, once again I'm observing the notepads next to me. I won't send you anything else after this, of that I promise, but know that I haven't finished my research. Next time you get that feeling that someone is behind you, watching. That is me. The next time you feel a shiver down your spine, that's me. The next time your ears burn, I'm talking to my notebook about all the plans I have for you. Every feeling you experience is a direct result of my actions; you are like my puppet. I'm pulling your strings, making you feel and act in certain ways. In a word, you're like my possession, I will have you one day, I'll make sure of that.

So, what can you do with this information. You could go to the police, but remember these papers were hand delivered to you. It might not be the brightest idea you've had. You could try and do it secretly, but you don't know what I look like or where I might be watching from. Maybe I'm a police officer, maybe I'm the homeless person at the end of the street, I could be both or none of these.

Let me make one thing clear. I have others out here with me, people who understand me. People who help and support me with my work. People who suggest new things for me to try. I'm saving some of my more special ideas for people like you. People who live their mundane lives, the same routine, day in and day out. People who, by no fault of their own, are the most boring people in existence. At least with people like you, I can make your life useful in assisting me with some pleasure. At least your life won't have been in vain.

Every time I see you, I get a flutter of anticipation of how I may feel when the time comes, how I'll do it and how satisfied you'll make me.

Even now, as I write this, I am filled with excitement. Don't worry, we are coming to an end, and I would like you to get some of your chores done on that long list you have.

Please think carefully before you act. Take everything into consideration whilst weighing up your options. Hand me over with the risk of repercussions, like I said before, I know people who are always willing to assist me. Or leave it as it is and let the remainer of your life play out. Who knows how long you'll have left, it could be days, weeks, months or even years. I could make you wait out the remainder of your natural days, keeping you on edge. I'll watch as your anxiety levels go to extremes, thinking each day you wake up might be your last. Each time you hear a noise your heart will pound with fear and terror as the blood rushes through your body thinking that that moment will be the end. I have a smile on my face just thinking about the emotions and reactions going through your mind. Well, I think I have rambled on enough. I just feel so passionately about what I do and just wanted you to get to know me in a way others haven't. Just before I let you ponder and go about your day, I just want to let you know, I've left a message hidden especially for you in these pages. You probably didn't notice whilst reading through, because of how scared and shocked you are. Have a breather, make yourself that brew you enjoy, you know the one I mean. I can smell it already as the steam escapes the mug. Come back and see if you can identify it. I'll give you a hint, the first letter of each paragraph spells out my special memo. I hope you have a pleasant day and night, get some rest and know that everything will work out the way it is supposed to.

Follow Matt and his work here:

AENIGMA MORTIS

BY

ELI BEALS

She was greeted by a sheriff at the crime scene tape, a welcome presence in any circumstance. His imposing stature guaranteed that none would cross the line if they were not meant to, yet his warmth was evident in his smile as Detective Artemis Tenon approached. She didn't go by her full name; she hated it when anyone other than her immediate family used it. To everyone else she was just Arty, or Tenon respectively.

"Got here fast Tenon, it's a weird one." Midas said in his deep baritone while lifting the yellow plastic barrier out of courtesy.

"Yeah, I was up already. Could use some coffee though."

"Don't worry I've got you covered." Midas made the call for immediate caffeine support and resumed securing the perimeter.

"Thanks Midas." Arty said as she approached the scene in full view.

A pair of garish neon green and pink running shoes, feet included, sat in the bright swath of a flood lamp.

As if someone had been on an early morning run to have their feet sliced clean off mid stride while the rest of them carried on.

She would have to wait for the lab guys and coroner to arrive, but she got herself a good hard look at the grim display.

Her initial observations told her that the shoes and socks were dressed postmortem as no blood could be seen on them or anywhere near, so whatever happened, happened elsewhere.

She assumed it was a female, due to the delicate bone structure, size and style of shoe.

"Black, two sugars." She heard over her shoulder and graciously accepted the proffered cup.

"Thanks." She said, never taking her gaze from the scene.

"No problem, what do you think this means?"

"No idea."

"Well, I don't like it, feels like the start of something bad y'know?"

"Yeah, I get that feeling too Midas." She said, regarding the severed feet thoughtfully while sipping her coffee.

Back in her office, surrounded by reports and photos that seemed to tell her exactly what she already knew but in much more detail. A vague timeline had been established that suggested the time of death somewhere between three or four weeks as the body had been preserved by freezing. While DNA was much faster these days it still took time and didn't always reveal who they were because there would have to be something in the database to compare it to. In the meantime, she contented herself by searching through recent missing persons cases, starting local, then expanding out. So far, she had a list of a dozen women, ages twenty-five to thirty.

To her relief, this search was reduced to one as DNA came back with a positive ID. Sydney McAllister; a prostitute with a light jacket, mostly minor things such as petty theft and drug possession with intent to distribute. As well as a missing person's report issued February 14th, almost three weeks ago, Valentine's Day. A mule, the ideal prey, an accessible nobody that wouldn't be missed.

The girl in the picture looked a touch older than herself when all she had to worry about was her upcoming trig exam, and when she could finally be rid of her braces. What future Sydney McAllister could possess had been denied her, and the empty sparkless eyes could only hint at the nature of its cruelty. Leaving her with the only choice she thought she had.

So far, this was looking like a single breadcrumb, and she would just have to wait for more to drop.

A familiar knock at her office doorway snapped her attention back to the forefront, and she let the mugshot settle to her desk.

"We got another one, Arty." Captain Stewart said, looking severe as usual. As she went to retrieve the detail sheet he stopped her with a look of concern.

"If this is what I think it is, we're not gonna have any problems like the last time the feds got involved right?"

"Of course not." She smiled while beckoning him to just hand it over.

Captain Stewart rolled his eyes while relinquishing the printout, not fooled by that smile one bit.

"As long as they aren't total assholes about it." Arty muttered.

"You know they always are." He said walking away then stopped abruptly and turned, holding a finger up. "Just play nice, okay?"

She replied with her best agreeable smile enjoying the look of resignation on the old Captain's face.

The assignment sheet was the same callout as the last one indicating a body or part of one had been discovered.

This time she arrived after the lab guys did, and they were waiting on her to clear the scene.

Nailed to the door of an apartment was a tongue in place of where a knocker would be.

"It's human, that's for sure. Unless sheep and goats are going for body piercing these days." She said noting the small divot near its center that indicated a barbell had once adorned it.

"The tenant called it in after he accidentally grabbed it thinking it was some kind of prank." The responding officer reported to her. Then added. "We're knocking on doors to see if anyone saw anything, so far nothing."

"I want to check this against those feet to see if we're looking at the same victim." The CSI Supervisor said to her. Then to a nearby colleague he said, "And we're going to have to cut the tongue from the door so we don't damage any trace." They hurried off to retrieve a saw and some release forms for the damage they were about to do.

"Any ideas?"

"Well, like the feet, this was sliced from the victim, post-mortem, probably a surgical saw, and due to the precise cut. I would say that it was frozen while they cut it."

"Same as the feet."

"Yup, as to the cause, well, so far we haven't ruled out murder."

"She went missing about three weeks ago." Arty said incredulously. "C'mon a girl in her line of work, it's the most likely scenario."

"Or she died of natural causes for our perp to discover and do this to her… Desecration of a corpse is still a felony Detective Tenon." He said looking her in the eyes over the rims of his glasses. He wasn't scolding her, just maintaining an objectivity so many have difficulty with one person in particular, herself.

"You're right." She sighed, allowing her convictions to pass, making way for any, and all possibilities, however unlikely.

"You'll know more as soon as we do Detective." He said with a slight smile.

"Thanks Bill." She said as she headed back to her SUV feeling tired, but she had one more stop to make before she was willing to call it a day.

There were a couple notorious locales synonymous with prostitution in her city, colloquially known as Tricksville, or the hotspot. Several hourly rate no tell motels served as hubs for business. As Arty pulled into the lot of one such place, she had already marked several women and a few men as on the clock.

As soon they noticed her they made themselves scarce. The ones that didn't scramble usually had something to say anyway, she thought to herself.

After about a dozen head shakes and blank stares she found one spark of recognition in a pair of eyes, a tall woman in a tight leopard print cocktail napkin-size skirt with heels that one could rotisserie a chicken on.

"She's dead, isn't she?" The woman known as Angel asked leaning over to see the picture Arty held out under the streetlamp.

"Yes, did you know her?"

"Like all hookers know each other huh?"

"You mean you don't?" She could give the sass as well as she could take it.

"Nah, I know her, names Cindy or somethin?

"Sydney, yeah close enough. Do you recall seeing her about three weeks ago?"

She divined this information by staring up at the night sky, invoking her last memory of Ms. McAllister. After a moment she clicked her tongue and brought that casual gaze back down to Arty.

“Yeah, it was Valentine’s Day, busy night. Was wearing a cute fur trim coat, saw her get into a car with some white guy. Only saw his hand outside the window. Car was nice, Mercedes.”

“A white guy driving a Mercedes, that narrows it down.”

At this Angel laughed. “I know right?”

“Ever seen it before?”

“Nah, but it's weird, most of us know better than to get into cars like that. But Cindy did, maybe he was loaded, I dunno. Oh, I forgot, the plates were Nevada plates, I remember now.”

“Nevada plates.” She jotted this down on her very short list of details.

Knowing this was as much as she was going to get from this excursion she handed Angel her card with the usual request. Stay safe, don't get into any cars, and if you see it again, please call me.

At this point, not even coffee would keep her going. The station was only a mile away so that's where the closest thing to a proper bed was for her, and fifteen minutes later she was quietly snoring on her office couch for just such an occasion.

When she awoke the sun was up again, just barely peeking over the low hills. She stretched and went to the washroom to splash some cold water on her face and brush her teeth.

She had two texts waiting for her, one from DNA saying the two samples were an exact match confirming that the two scenes were connected. She was both relieved and perplexed by this news as it did not indicate a Serial Killer was on the loose, but that someone had butchered this woman and were staging parts of her over the city.

The second text announced that another body part was found on the steps of the downtown library and had since been collected and that she was welcome to visit the morgue at her nearest convenience.

She always liked the morgue, for one thing it was quiet. The kind of quiet that demanded a certain level of reverence in the same way a library or holy ground does. This sacred space was Dr. Surya Jain's domain which he tended to with the fastidiousness of a Benedictine monk.

"I knew right away that more than just her eyes were missing." Dr. Jain said more to the severed head than to Arty. Hefting it easily as if to demonstrate the anomaly.

"The average human head weighs about eight pounds, this one is five point one."

"So, the brain is missing?"

"Excerebration, the process of removing the brain for embalming. The ethmoid bone is punched through via the nasal cavity and the brain is blended up or liquefied and pulled out with a metal hook. Of all the organs the Egyptians preserved, the brain was not considered necessary to bring with them to the afterlife." He mused, oblivious to Artys indifference.

She knew better than to interrupt his esoteric explanations, so she just let him expound until the relevant information was forthcoming. Which turned out to be inconclusive, as not enough of her was present to determine any cause of death. His only parting comfort was that all deaths are due to asphyxiation, where the brain is deprived of oxygen by any number of causes.

Back in her office she had reduced the three scenes to single images arranged on her wall. Willing some pattern or significance to the selected body parts to reveal the message.

Her talk with Doctor Jain had her thinking in the line of ritual symbolism and went on a deep dive into the web, central to these particular items.

Nothing seemed to click. Whatever this was she concluded after six hours of screen time, that it either meant nothing or that she would just have to wait.

She didn't have to wait long.

Since the case had become active, the call center had been inundated with calls involving viscera found in unlikely places. Some of these were disregarded but anything resembling a genuine connection was filtered to her cell phone. Her first site was a pile of organs on the side of a service road which turned out to be deer, followed by a bloody patch of hair in a grocery store parking lot that was also not human. She suspected that someone had hit a stray dog somewhere and merely discarded what was still stuck to their vehicle.

Her next callout was to one of the nicer suburbs, the kind that rarely have cars parked streetside, the kind of place kids on Halloween would flock to for full sized candy bars.

This particular home was all ninety degree angles hugging huge panes of glass, tinted so that if anyone looked in could only glean a vague sense of its opulence.

Arty made her way to the master bedroom to be once again met by a scene that resonated with her case. A large bed, fashioned to appear that it was hovering by some kind of futuristic technology, sat as the room's centerpiece. An interesting feature, except it was overshadowed by the pair of eyes positioned a few inches apart onto the snow white pillows like pale meatballs on small coils of spaghetti.

"Think it was the Central Valley Butcher?" Midas asked.

"Hmm?" Arty said absently, immersed in her observations.

"That's what they're calling him."

"Oh, yeah, definitely him." She wasn't looking at the pair of disgorged eyes arranged atop one of the two pillows, but intently at the painting hung over the bed. What drew her attention to it was that it was slightly askew.

"Anyone touch this?"

"No." Midas said, his eyebrows raised curiously as she breezed by him.

She pathed from one room to another, aiming her flashlight at the walls and various sculptures that adorned the place. Then, as if certain of something, she nodded as if checking a mental box she headed back to the master bedroom where Midas still stood, his expression unchanged.

"This one doesn't fit. It's not like anything else in the house. The frame, the subject, is just wrong." She said, hitting the painting with her light for emphasis.

"I don't follow."

"All the other art is generic minimalist stuff, meant to fit the color scheme… decorations, this clashes. I don't think the homeowner put it here, I think it was this Butcher. Who called this one in, by the way?"

"The maid. The man of the house is away but supposed to return later today."

She continued to ponder the out of place artwork, there was something familiar about it that she couldn't quite place and so it occupied her focus for some time. It was a landscape on plain unadorned canvas, depicting a wide curve of a river. The point of view was from the shade in a grove of oak trees. At the far bank, almost to the painting's left edge was a small boat with a figure with their back turned as if heading back to land. In the distance, and clearly the most prominent object of the piece spanned a green painted bridge.

She was still looking at it when the crime lab arrived, she was slightly disappointed when it wasn't Bill. His input would have been interesting regarding this painting she thought.

He'd probably make some witty comment about it being "quite eye catching", or something like that, she thought groaning inwardly at her own terrible pun.

As for the eyes, all but forgotten in her examination of the painting she would learn that they had been removed while the victim was still alive, which made this a murder. Though her assumption was correct, this was by no means a signpost as to the killer's identity.

The resident of the house had arrived just as they were wrapping up and was more than a little irritated that he had all these people milling around his property.

He calmed down a bit after he was informed of the situation and thoroughly confused about the painting in his room.

"It's not mine." He said dismissively as he seemed more concerned about the absence of his bedding set.

"We'll get those back to you as soon as we can." She said, doing her level best to seem cordial.

"Clean I hope?"

"Uh, yeah sure." Arty said, confident enough to pass his scrutiny.

After a brief and unproductive exchange with Mr. Lyle, Arty headed back to the station to do some serious reconnaissance on local topography. Specifically the river.

The Sacramento River is four hundred miles north to south, while many bridges span it only one was painted green that she could tell. The Jibboom Street bridge. Similarities were evident from the image search and the depiction in the painting that had been brought to her office by request.

Arranged in sequence she had pictures of the feet, the tongue, the head, and the eyes tacked up on a corkboard next to the painting.

Captain Stewert knocked on her open-door frame looking as if he'd been standing there for a good while.

“How's it going Tenon?”

She gestured a teetering motion with her hand and sighed. “It's like there's something here staring me in the face with an idea. And I can't see it.”

“Overthinking it perhaps?” He said as he faced the arrangement before her. “Quite the rebus.” He mused after a moment.

“A what?”

“A puzzle or riddle with images instead of words.”

“Riddle?” She sprung up, suddenly charged with energy.

“What can run, but never walks?” She pointed to the feet.

“What has a mouth but cannot speak.” She said before he could reply.

“The tongue.” Stewart's eyes widened and continued. “What has a head and cannot think?” She tapped the photo of the eyeless and brainless head.

“The eyes are in a bed… and the eyes are staring up at the ceiling, sleepless, and there's the answer.” Pointing at the painting.

“A river. Yeah.”

“Full circle, that bridge is only a half a click away from where we found the feet. Something is there, I know it.”

Captain Stewart nodded and set off a flurry of activity calling as much support this operation could possibly need.

The presence of police activity naturally drew crowds. A large gathering of curious citizens and more than a couple news vans packed the sparse parking lot and adjacent side streets. While they watched in rabid fascination, they were unaware that they were being watched right back. Killers often return to see and experience the chaos they had created, and so Arty scanned the group bordering the shore to see if any of them struck a chord. Anyone that looked even slightly suspicious would be given a closer look, but nothing stood out to her so she boarded the awaiting boat that would join several others out on the water for the search.

It didn't take long to find the body. The dive team were under only a few minutes until one emerged with a thumbs up. To the vigilant onlookers' collective morbid delight, a black plastic clad form emerged from the river bottom.

Arty knew immediately it was Sydney McAllister and it would be a while before she could learn anything from her retrieval so she directed the driver of the boat to head to another part of the river further west just before the American river met the Sacramento river.

"What about the body?" The driver asked, gesturing towards the bridge.

"Trust me on this okay." She replied and nodded west, away from the primary scene. He obliged without another word.

The spot she was looking for was where the figure in the painting had made landfall.

By the time they found the approximate location it was getting dark, and sure enough, peeking beneath some brush she saw it without the need for a light.

"He wanted this found." She said thinking aloud as she hopped to shore. She remembered to glove up before touching anything, but it was unlikely the Butcher had left anything to trace back to him, careful as he had been already.

Inside a battered steel tackle box amongst some rusty fishhooks and ancient bait was a folded sheet of paper. There was a single word printed on the page, *BOOM*.

A sudden explosion cracked through the evening air, echoing up the river.

She whipped around to catch sight of burning debris falling in glowing contrails amidst a thick column of smoke. The officer that had accompanied her uttered an exclamation in shocked disbelief. A strange feeling washed over her, something that bordered on anger and pure animal terror as she watched the smoke blow away in the evening breeze.

Four deaths and dozens injured, three of them severe and in critical condition was the total count. Arty sat buried in her work which served as insulation against the tidal wave of grief she felt. Faces of her colleagues smiled up at her from personnel files beside the crime scene photos. Friends, now reduced to victims. When she looked up, she saw Captain Stewart approaching from down the hall, thankful for a few seconds to brush away the tears collecting in her eyes.

"Our Butcher has been promoted to terrorist it seems, you know what this means right?" Captain Stewart said wearily.

"Jumping to conclusions, are we?" Tenon said with a slight smile.

"That's what the media will say about it. Journalists used to wait for facts in times long past." He mused, his expression wistful. "They are still collecting body parts, and so far they're convinced the bomb was detonated remotely. No timer. Feds will be here today."

"Yeah, don't worry. Honestly, I could use some help." She said, but this was only half true. Several people she knew were dead, and at this point it didn't matter to her how the Butcher was caught, only that he would be, and soon.

"And Tenon, I'm glad you're okay, but I'm wondering why the Butcher didn't bomb both sites?"

"Because I solved the riddle, it's my reward, he wants to keep playing."

“Yeah, that's what worries me. Be careful out there, alright?”

“No promises.” She said quietly as he left.

She took his cue and called it a day. The idea of a hot bath, a glass of red wine and a trashy novel sounded really good. The Feds would just have to go without a formal welcome on her part, she told herself.

Something wasn't right, she thought as she pulled into her car park. The porchlight was out, not in and of itself strange, yet as she approached the door, she had drawn her weapon with her thumb tensing on the safety.

The door was slightly ajar, and then her automatic was live and ready to fire.

“I'm armed! Anyone in there come out with your hands up!” She yelled from the cover of a wide tapered support post. At the count of five she burst into her living room immediately clearing spaces she knew anyone could be hiding in.

Heart racing, she followed the sights of her pistol, systematically checking every room until she was satisfied then called it in.

Maybe she had just left the door open, and the porchlight simply burned out, maybe, maybe not.

Due to the recent events she had to assume that there would be a bomb somewhere, so she waited for backup outside behind her SUV while never taking her eyes from the condo. She only relented her vigilance when her street was flooded with red and blue flashing lights, the cavalry had arrived.

After giving a brief statement, she began to knock on her nearby neighbors doors to ask if anything seemed suspicious, which yielded not much save for a weekend barbeque invite. Twenty minutes after that, the bomb sniffing dogs and their handlers were departing with an all clear so that the rest of the waiting investigators could proceed.

She learned that the intruder entered through the sliding glass patio door and had most likely exited through the front, and that her porchlight had indeed burned out in its natural course of life.

"I prefer incandescent myself as well." Bill said as he was sorting through a stack of envelopes then stopped at one in the pile.

"I'm sorry, what?" She was only half listening.

"Incandescent light output is the full spectrum of light, including infrared, that's why they feel warmer. Plus, I just like the classics. I believe this letter was hand delivered to you Detective."

He held it out for her to see. She didn't recognize the sender, nor the florid handwriting that looped and swirled across its face.

"Aenigma Mortis? What kind of name is that?" She asked.

"It's not a name, at least I don't think so, it means riddle of death in Latin."

"And it's not postmarked."

“Very good Detective. We're gonna have this analyzed and will keep you posted.” He said with a cheeky smirk and bagged the letter as evidence.

As her home was now a crime scene, she would have to defer that bath and wine for a shower and another night on her office couch.

She gave the condo a last look before setting off, thinking how it was somehow tainted, a place she associated with safety and familiarity had now become threatening and uninhabitable. She wasn't sure that she could return until this Aenigma Mortis was apprehended.

Sure, they would assign some officers to keep an eye on her place while she was there, but this violation of her sanctuary would not allow her to rest.

Her office bore a new feature, an FBI agent, who stood surveying her display of breadcrumbs, amongst those lay the letter and envelope collected and analyzed on her desk.

He turned to face her as she entered bowing slightly, sensing she was in no mood for anything other than a quick introduction.

“Special Agent Ben Harken. Just came in from DC. Heard about your ordeal, I'm sorry.”

She didn't respond immediately as she was somewhat taken aback by his manner. Professional and neatly dressed yet humble in a way that belied her experience with his particular agency.

“Yeah, thanks, Arty Tenon.” She shook his hand that he had held out to her in greeting.

“I won't take up any more of your time, I'm sure you're exhausted.” He said, noting her longing glance at the couch. Just one thing though, that note you've got there?”

“Yes?”

“You're not the first one to get one of those.”

Her expression remained passive, but her eyes lit with a burning curiosity, urging him to continue.

“Eight years ago, in Massachusetts. Same handwriting, same two pence stamp from the late eighteen hundreds.”

“Same killer.” She said, deflating a bit, knowing for certain that her case was now officially federal.

“Yeah, I know you want to catch this guy, so do I. I think we can help each other Detective, I'm not here to steamroll you. Goodnight.” He said as he turned to the door and left.

After a brief struggle to leave it till morning, she went to her desk to read the letter. Unlike the precise and elegant script, the note seemed penned in a greater hurry. The lines, more erratic and jagged but still identifiable as the same author as on the envelope.

It read:

Greetings detective, You are doing quite well, but that was an easy one. Things will only get harder for you I'm afraid. I must air a bit of a grievance. The news is calling me the Central Valley Butcher. I've always hated those names they've branded me with, so unimaginative, don't you agree? It's always Strangler, Ripper or Axeman, I kind of liked that one though.

In a way we are working together, so I ask as a professional courtesy to refer to me as Aenigma Mortis, or perhaps just The Enigma. Im looking forward to our next little adventure.

Sir Arthur Conan Doyle wrote, When you have eliminated all that is impossible, then whatever remains, however improbable, must be the truth.

Catch me if you can.

The pleasant tone and subtle menace of the note left her stunned for a while as she considered the implications. Impossible ideas slid through her mind and vanished into the void of superstition until she took a deep breath and let it out slowly. She was again calm, relaxed, and then she uttered through the plate glass and to the darkness beyond: "Okay then, I will."

Follow Eli and his work here:

Serial Killers

INTERVIEW WITH A SERIAL KILLER

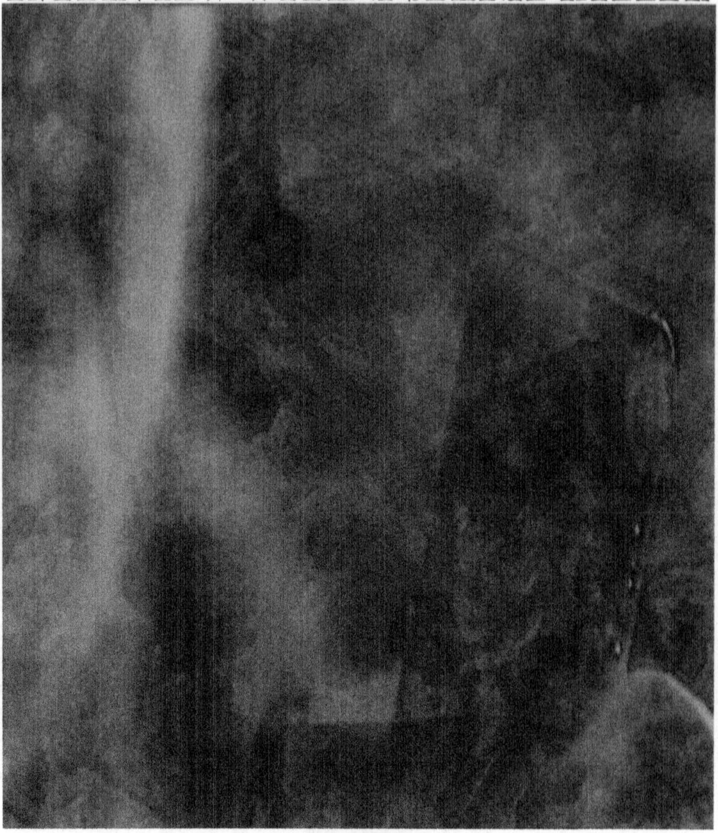

BY
STEPHEN KNIGHT

Serial Killers

Can someone please tell me how many people you have to kill before you fall into that category of being a serial killer? I mean, one probably makes you an opportunist. Two? Okay, you may have got the taste for it. Three. Yes. It must be three. Yes. Three. Although Jack the Ripper was the first real known famous serial killer and he did five. I would have loved to have seen his victims. Didn't he gut them? Mutilate them beyond recognition? How he would have felt now. All that recognition. All those books and films. But then, he would have been enjoying the recognition. The acknowledgement of his power and control over those prostitutes. There was no television. It wasn't as if he could have said that he was going to be starring in a film starring someone like Brad Pitt cast as him. Or even being featured on one of those *'World's Greatest Serial Killer's'* programmes on Tubi or Pluto, analysed by some criminal psychologist whose only expertise is that he or she has read it right out of a book and is being paid to sit there and look like a complete twat.

They don't understand, you know. They never do. No. Never understand. They sit there listing things about how you came from a broken family with physical or sexual abuse, family dysfunction, emotionally distant or absent parents, how you were a loner who watched pornography, participated in martial arts, was obsessed by guns. And everyone believes them! Yes! Everyone believes what they don't actually know about you. The power of the media. You look at what they said about that poor guy Christopher Jefferies. He was an intelligent man who preferred his own company and had his own selection of close friends. Yet the media ruined him. They called him 'The Nutty Professor', 'weird' and 'creepy'. 'Unmarried oddball' who was 'obsessed with death.' My God, even I feel sorry for him. If it were me, I would have gone out and killed someone just to live up to what they were accusing me of.

I hope that I get the notoriety I deserve. I have because I am here with you, I'm not afraid to tell you everything. But I must say the Police were so slow. So close. They even knocked on my door when doing house to house enquiries. They asked all the right questions; where I was at a certain time, can they have a look around my house. Ha-ha. Twats.

I remember some of my neighbours describing me just how the press described poor Christopher. I am that weird, creepy unmarried oddball who is obsessed with death. Not my death. The death of those around me. The neighbours told the Police.

Do I get a thrill from killing? Pleasure? See what you think. How many did I kill? Let's just say enough to be deemed a serial killer. How does that make me feel? Powerful. Because when you are stood over the body, the result of your frenzy, you know that they cannot harm you as much as if they were alive. You want to carry on. My main pleasure was standing there, when I knew that I was unlikely to be disturbed and I would masturbate over the body or, as the case might be, have sex with the victim. What is it they call that? Ah, yes. Necrophilia. The Police no doubt took samples but when you aren't known to them and have never committed a crime, or I might add, been caught before, they have no record of you. You will always never be found until you make a mistake.

So let me see. At last count, I think it was five. All women. All blondes. I have a thing for blondes. What a beautiful colour, especially if it is natural. Not those ones who feel the need to try and make themselves beautiful by dyeing their hair every couple of weeks. It's usually to hide their grey hair. They have a thing about not wanting to appear old.

So five. The first one wasn't planned. Well perhaps it was. She was nearing sixteen and so was I. Both of us went to St Margaret's school in Plymouth. School wasn't good for me. I was bullied, not that I want that to be an excuse, because what I have done now makes me more powerful than those bullies could ever be. I was called a fat cunt, regularly pinned against the wall by the same gang containing both male and females and my lunch money taken, my schoolbooks thrown on the floor and trodden on or ripped up. One day as I was on the floor being kicked I noticed her. She was blonde. My eyes pierced her. I didn't care about the others. In a way I was obsessed from then. Before that, she was just one of the bullies. She had only participated in the emotional abuse. Now she had gone that one step further. She was physical, kicking and thumping me. Just her hair, her eyes filled with hate. Yes. I was obsessed.

I saw her outside of school some weeks later. She was on her own. I started following her. I found out where she lived. I remember seeing a woman at her door, even more beautiful than her. I think it was her mother. I fantasised about fucking the both of them Individually and both together. I undressed them with my eyes and psychologically felt their naked skin, their breasts and body rubbing up against me. I remember walking around the side of their house and peering through the window at the both of them. The didn't see me. But I stood there masturbating. My thoughts had made me too excited. That was the first pleasure that I got from Rachel Cole and her mother.

From then on, I regularly waited for her, followed her, bought the same things as her just so I could taste what she was eating and drinking. She bought some sexy underwear one day in Ann Summers. She didn't see me. I was over the other side of the store looking at the sex toys. Wondering about how I could use them on her. She bought a very revealing bra and crotchless panties. It was obvious that she was going to wear them on Valentines Day for her boyfriend, another boy who had abused me at school, Michael Dickenson. As she left, I bought exactly the same outfit. The assistant looked at me kinda weird and told me that the underwear was the second set that she had sold that day and it was the girl who has just left who had bought the other. I don't participate in friendly conversation so just paid for the goods and left. I enjoyed wearing the bra and panties on many an occasion from then.

It was early evening on a Saturday. The sun was just setting so it was getting dark about 8pm. I was watching her. She left her house in Greenwood Park Road and went down the back lane. I guessed that she was going to her boyfriend. Well, that is what they said in the newspapers and on the headlines on the TV. It was quiet. No one around. I had taken my dad's posh kitchen knife. He has a set of them because he is a chef. He had just bought a new set for work and so we had the leftovers. Boy, they were sharp. You could drop a piece of paper on it and the paper would just separate. Ironic that they describe the knife as 'The slicing, dicing and mincing multitasker' ha-ha. Because that is exactly what I did to her. I ran up behind her. She didn't hear me. She had her headphones in. The adrenaline was pumping in my body, I could feel the excitement, I could feel myself already wanting to laugh. I had control. I had power over the girl that destroyed my confidence. I stabbed her several times in the back. She fell to the floor face first. I turned her over. Her eyes widened as she saw my face. I smiled and then laughed but said nothing as she tried to scream. I didn't give her a chance. I must have stabbed her about thirty times. When I knew that she was dead, I cut some of her hair and took it home. I still have it! I stripped the dead, bloodied body and from her bag took out the sexy underwear that she had bought. Carefully I dressed her in it. I took photos of her corpse on my phone. Here! I still wank over the photo's now and again whilst wearing the same underwear that I purchased.

So … well. The Police thought that the culprit was her boyfriend. She had told her friends at school that they had been arguing a lot recently and that the underwear was a last-ditch attempt to renew their relationship. They arrested him. He couldn't give an alibi for where he was. He was remanded. If anything, it taught him a lesson. Word is out that he was raped several times in the young offender's place. So. I had control. I had power. That's what my first kill was all about. Teaching them a lesson.

So, am I insane? I don't think so. Most serial killers aren't. Some serial killers display symptoms of mental illnesses such as psychosis or bipolar disorder I believe. We are known to be highly intelligent. After Rachel, I did three A Levels and had A+ grades in all three. I went to university and studied, would you believe, Psychology. I got a first. I have an IQ of 129. The killing of the girl gave me my confidence and self-esteem back. Like I said. Control and power.

It was five years before I had the urge to get some excitement in my life again. I kept myself to myself at university. But one night I met a girl completely by accident. She was struggling with her shopping in one arm and trying to push her pushchair in the other and control a toddler at the same time. Me? I was feeling alone. I saw her, blonde hair and so I instantly started to get excited. It had been five years. I carried her bags for her. I couldn't take my eyes off her hair, her face. I had seen her before. She lived along the street where my student digs were in Exeter. As we approached her house, I could tell that she was feeling lonely as well because she invited me in. All I wanted to do was run my fingers through her hair.

After a coffee and a bit of time talking whilst watching the TV that was on in the background, she indicated that it was time for her to put the toddler to bed and then breastfeed the baby before laying him down in his cot. The older kid was so good. Cleaned his teeth as he was told and then went to bed. I could hear Marly reading to her son before she returned back downstairs where I was waiting. It was so sudden. She did it like she didn't care. At first, I felt embarrassed by her just undoing her top and her maternity bra and letting the breast drop down. I stared at her free breast as the baby soon latched on. The embarrassment was soon replaced by excitement. I could feel it in my pants. My penis was starting to get erect, and I had no way to hide it and so I leaned forward. I kept looking in a way that made it look like I was looking at the baby. As an excuse I thought I would take the empty coffee cups back out to the kitchen. There I saw the glimmer of the knife on the rack. There were five in total. Nothing as exquisite as the one I used on Rachel, but still, I could hear the voices calling to me, demanding that I pick the biggest one.

Marly never stood a chance. She was more interested in the baby crying then my return to the living room. I walked in forcefully and just swiped the blade across her neck. She dropped the kid on the floor. Obviously, the kid was in pain from the fall because it started crying uncontrollably. I didn't stop. I jumped on top of the woman and just thrust the knife into her stomach, her torso and her arms randomly. There was no logistical positioning of the knife. She desperately tried to stop both the blood gushing from the wound on her neck and stop any more knife wounds. The blade at one point lunged through her left hand. She never had the power to push me off. Her life-force was leaving her body faster than the bullet train in Japan. The number of stab wounds? I lost count. I was more interested, once Marly's body stopped struggling with what little life she had left, in shutting the baby up. Not only was it getting on my nerves, but I had to stop it crying in case it alerted the neighbours. I looked into Marly's eyes and reached down to run my fingers through her hair. She looked so calm. So innocent. So scared. I really wanted to fuck her. I lifted her dress and ripped her panties off. They instantly got stuffed into my pocket on my trousers whilst at the same time I loosened the buckle on the belt on my pants and undid my jeans. I had to do it. Fucking a dead body is just so relieving. They are so tight. I didn't last long as I did get over excited.

The baby? No, don't be silly. If there's something I am not and that is a paedophile. I wouldn't fuck a child. What do you take me for? But the fucking thing wouldn't stop screaming. I picked it up. I was covered in blood. It was all over my hands and each time I tried to stop the kid crying the blood dripped down onto its face and onto its lips. I think the kid enjoyed the taste because it started to lick its lips. The thought did cross my mind of giving it some more of its mother's blood. For whatever reason I had it in my head that the baby was a witness. My god it was about four months old, and my thoughts were totally senseless. But I couldn't stop it screaming. I threw the little girl across the room until it hit the far wall. I was shouting at it to shut the fuck up. But it didn't. If anything, it was in more pain. It started gurgling as though it were choking.

I stopped to think. Stared down at my sexual conquest and then back in the direction of the screaming child. Then I stormed over to the far wall, crouched down and with the knife I stabbed the baby over and over and over again until its life was extinct. I probably stabbed it more times than I had its mother. But my conscience was clear. I didn't care. It had shut up. I had the control back. I had the power. I leaned over Marly and with the knife I cut a clump of her blonde hair and stuffed it into the opposite pocket from the panties. I had my trophies.

So, what about the kid upstairs? He had seen me. Could he recognise me? Would he be at an age where he could describe me, do a photofit or pick me out in a line up? I had to make the decision to let him live or give him the same fate as his mother. He would probably be frightened, seeing me stood in the doorway brandishing a bloodied knife. But remember, fear doesn't stop death, it stops life. You see, the things we fear the most have already happened to us. At his age he was too young to even experience fear. The worst thing that had happened to him was the fear of losing his teddy bear after he had thrown it out of the highchair for fuck's sake.

He was lucky. There was a noise outside. Someone banged on the door. I froze. All the lights were on in the house making it look like someone was home, yet no one was answering. Now I knew at this point that the hardest part for me was going to be able to get away without being seen. She had a back door. Perhaps there was a way out of the back. I only lived down the road. I had to take the chance. I made it. The kid survived to live another day. The one that got away.

The next day the murders were all over the news. Young Ritchie had come down to find his mother in the middle of the night, had reached down to cuddle the dead woman and the blood had covered him. He opened the front door and headed out into the street. One of the students coming back from a night on the town found him about half a mile away in just his underpants and plastered in blood. What is this world coming to? A four-year-old child can walk all that distance before being noticed?

The Police knocked on doors everywhere. They didn't even suspect me. You tell a young officer that you were home all night apart from going to the shops and he believes you. The CCTV from the shop confirmed exactly what I said, and there was no chance of there being any CCTV in the street where I lived because it was so run down. Even if there was, they would have probably vandalised it. I had an alibi, yes.

Well. Turns out that Marly was only a prostitute. She used to leave her kids alone whilst she went out to do her business. So, she probably deserved to die. Two out of three ain't bad. Richie may have had a better life, who knows, thanks to me. If you take the psychological profiles of serial killers from those TV psychologists I mentioned earlier, then young Richie is the perfect fit to follow in my footsteps. Childhood experiences, dysfunctional family environments, and psychological trauma is a starting point.

Do I have a conscience about killing the baby? The answer is no. She would never know his father. She was a bastard. Let's face it, Marly probably didn't know who the father was herself if she was a prostitute. It could have been any man from a long list. So maybe I did her a favour.

Do you know that in each of my kills, my heart rate has increased immensely with the level of excitement I get? It's a magical feeling, believe me. The dopamine in my brain must have been working overtime. It makes me laugh as I realise just what a sadistic bastard I am, and I couldn't give a fuck. But then, you would probably tell me that my typical lack of empathy, desire for control, and a fascination with death and violence is responsible for that.

Let's get on to number four. Would it be number four? Does the baby count? I mean it's only a fucking baby. If my modus operandi were that I like to kill blondes, and the baby wasn't blonde then would it count? Good question. Well for the purpose of this interview, we will count the baby in. So, number four.

I graduated. Managed to get a job in a solicitors of all places. Legal executive. Now that for one tells you that serial killers come from all walks of life. I remember reading a book called *'Picking Up the Pieces'* and in it the author mentions a man who had a makeshift court in the basement of his house. He was trialling rabbits. Yes, bloody rabbits. Cruel bastard. Thing is that their fate was sealed. Each one was found guilty and sent to the electric chair and electrocuted. Most of the time their bodies exploded, and the blood splattered all over the room. He never used to clean it up and the neighbours were complaining about the smell. The author, a criminal psychologist in both public and private practice wrote that due to patient confidentiality he couldn't report the acts to the authorities, but even if he could, the most that the nutter would get charged with is animal cruelty. But there was more to it. The man had been sexually abused by his stepfather for most of his life. The rabbits were each named after his stepfather, and he would convene the court each time he had bad memories. It was a coping mechanism. The author ends by saying that the victim is out walking the streets among other people just as you and I do. What I am trying to say is that you do not know the person in the street stood next to you at the pedestrian crossing, in the coffee shop, or even at work.

So, there I was, assisting a senior partner by defending exactly the sorts of people that I have become. Who better? To say I had personal experience, well, it was beneficial to the client. The bad thing was when they would come clean about their crimes, it was exciting. I used to get them to tell me more because I was enjoying it.

I was assigned to one of the senior partners, Deborah Piner. She was a right bitch. Found fault in everything I was doing, even down to inputting the wrong formula in an Excel spreadsheet. Complained about me in a partner meeting and demanded that I was swapped. I hated her as much as she hated me. At the moment she had the power and control. Don't you just hate the people who are in prominent positions in companies, so much so that they have their heads stuck up their own arses so far that surely it must hurt? The worst thing about it? Every time I sat opposite her I could feel my penis getting erect. It wasn't as if she turned me on. It was the colour of her hair. She was naturally blonde. I think that the day she complained about me was one of the days that she saw the bulge in my trousers. Who knows?

The Police need to think themselves lucky, because determining the motive in a serial murder investigation can be challenging, as a single killer may exhibit multiple motivations across their crimes. Working in the solicitors helped me see that what with our clients. There are seven; Power and control, revenge, sexual gratification, financial gain, attention and notoriety, thrill seeking, ideology or mission. I often used to sit at my desk analysing myself, quite pissed off that my profile only fitted five of those motivations. Power and control I love, perhaps sexual gratification in as much that I loved to fuck the victims, albeit after death and so far, only the one. I've already mentioned the attention and notoriety when I started. I think there is an element of thrill seeking. With Deborah Piner there was definitely an element of revenge.

Now this Deborah Piner. Here I was. I hated her, she hated me. Blonde hair. I knew that she was my next kill. The thrill for me was the fact that I would probably be the suspect from day one when the Police asked the other senior partners if there was anyone that they could think of who may have a grudge against Miss Piner. I think I would be first choice after her complaints. Looking back on it now, her being a victim was a bit close to home. The Police would do their homework. Rachel Cole: I was associated in some way. Marly Davidson: I lived in the same street. Now Deborah Piner: I worked with her. It would be three, okay four deaths, and if they looked close enough then the common denominator could be me. But I didn't give a fuck. The thrill was doing it and not getting caught with Deborah. It would give me the power and control I wanted.

Getting her home address was simple. I had access to everything being the legal executive. It was as simple as going into her office whilst she was at a meeting and checking her handbag for a letter she may have there. Easy. She was one of these people who thought that she was so important that she didn't even bother to open her own mail. But it also gave me a bit of a break. I wouldn't be the only suspect with an M. O. She had received her decree nisi from her husband's solicitors. Ironic that they were the company whose offices were directly next door on the Plymouth Barbican. So, another suspect emerges.

It was Wednesday. I overheard a telephone call. Deborah had invited her soon to be ex-husband over for dinner at 8pm on Friday that week in order that they could amicably discuss their divorce. Perfect. I knew that. I had two days to scout the area for CCTV, both inside the grounds of her house and outside on the street, although she lived in the middle of nowhere on Dartmoor. I decided to enter through the rear of the property, mainly because at the back she just had moorland filled with wild ponies and sheep. There was only one car in her driveway. I knew from eve's dropping in on conversations that her and her equally bitchy secretary had discussed that she didn't have children. She didn't want any. She wanted her career. I often thought that she may be a closet lesbian in reality, but then I thought that most lesbians were good fun to hang around.

I was well camouflaged. All in black. Black face mask around the bottom half of my face. I opened the patio door. It wasn't locked which confirmed just how arrogant this woman was. I walked in. I could hear her, banging pans in what I took to be the kitchen. She was stood peeling potatoes whilst looking out of the kitchen window onto the side garden.

I remember looking at her. From behind she was quite beautiful, slim, well-toned and that beautiful blonde hair which draped down her back. Some people have beauty on the inside as well as the outside. How you give it from the heart shows your beauty. How you treat others around you. This woman was just a horrible person on the outside. I needed to see if she had any beauty on the inside. Grasping the knife that I had originally used on Rachel Cole nearly six years earlier and kept as a trophy, I raised it above my head and struck it down into her back. She was screaming and reaching behind her head with both hands as though she were trying to remove it. I pilled the blade back out as she turned to face me, the masked man. But I needed her to see just who was purifying her. I pulled down the face cover and she recognised me instantly. Her eyes widened, her legs started to wobble like those of a giraffe when first born and then she fell backwards.

I didn't waste any time. I knew that her husband would be arriving soon. Her body was semi-conscious and, on the floor, although on the side. She was powerless. I rolled her over onto her back and then without any further warning I forced the knife into her heart, once, twice, three times. Her eyes stared up at me, lifeless, but just in case, I continued stabbing over and over again. I wasn't counting. I had to see the beauty if there was any. I started ripping the knife downwards and sideways with each blow. Surely if there was any beauty to be found then I would have found it by now. The blood was spurting out and flowing onto the kitchen floor. I could see her intestines and other organs. But there was no beauty. Apart from her hair, and even that was now red and no longer blonde. The woman was dead. Life extinct. Did I have time? Did I really want to fuck someone who was dead in real life. The answer was no. I had taken her life away. I had done the world a favour. Destroyed what very little beauty she possessed.

And that was it. Number four. What? I said five. Oh yes. I did, didn't I? Well let me see. What colour is your hair? Yes. Blonde. Why are you laid there, naked, with your hands tied? Well, Detective Inspector Williams, I hate to say this. But you are number five. You see, you can put me down in all the press conferences that you have held and front so confidently, describing me as a lonely psychopath, dangerous and uncaring. But you do not know the real me. Serial killers have been around for centuries. Locusta, a Roman woman hired by Agrippina the Younger, the mother of Nero, had to poison several members of the imperial family; Locusta was executed in 69 BC. Bluebeard was executed in the 15th century for the murder of more than 100 children. What did they both get? Notoriety.

Do you have the right me in your press conferences? Maybe. You will never know. I am that weird, creepy unmarried oddball who is obsessed with death. I am also obsessed with life. My life. Everyone thinks they know me. You are just as bad as those TV psychologists that describe the traits of the convicted serial killers. You stand up in front of those reporters with your profile. Face it, this time you even got that wrong. I have to be obsessed with my life. Because everybody else is.

So, number five, what am I going to do with you? You see, I could let you live. I have the power to do that. I am the one in control. I could make you be so paranoid that you are afraid to go outside, you are constantly looking over your shoulder wondering if I am there and your time is finally up. I could install the fear in you. Your confidence and self-esteem could be so low that you become a different person, just like I was at school all those years ago. You may be there wanting to arrest me, but I HAVE THE FUCKING POWER TO SAY IF AND WHEN YOU CAN! Perhaps we leave it to fate. The toss of a coin. Because that is what life is. The more we are aware of who we are and the sources of meaning in our lives, the wiser the decisions we will make. I am a serial killer. The only thing meaningful in my life at this moment in time is that I CONTROL THE SITUATION!

I stepped forward, knife prone. I still had to make that decision. Dead or alive. Either way I would fuck her. But then I looked down to my chest. Three red dots on my torso. I could attempt to kill number five. I still had the power over the situation. If I forced the knife into her heart, then chances are I would die. She might live. If I let her live by going down on my knees with my hands on my head just as I was being ordered to do, I had the control over the situation, but my power would have gone indirectly. Detective Inspector Williams would be psychologically damaged. Just like I have been since my time at school. I have power. I have control. This is Thomas-Jay Packer, Serial Killer, signing off.

Follow Stephen and his work here:

Serial Killers

RUINATION

BY
ARTHUR L

Serial Killers

"I hope the police find him very soon" Patrick said, and Christine agreed.

Police had been searching Christine's city for the killer going on three weeks already, with no luck and no leads.

Seven women had been murdered in that three-week period, leaving the population in a state of hysterical fear. It was almost certainly a man. He used a knife. A big, jagged, hunting knife. There was always a huge amount of blood at the place of each killing. A sadness hung over the city.

Christine was scared, and for one second no longer wanted to be in Patrick's new car with him. But that feeling passed quickly. It was their fifth date. Patrick was stylish and polite. And very handsome!

"Why don't we listen to the radio?" Patrick had asked a few minutes before. The mood was right, but three kisses into a love song, the DJ interrupted to announce that an eighth body had been found, with authorities confident it was the same killer as before.

There were multiple stab wounds, and while the victim's family had been notified, her name had not been released. The announcer said that she was identified by DNA, and her wallet and phone. Not by recognition of friends or family. Christine thought that was weird, for a moment.

The love song started up again. It was a good one.

They'd both noticed the sexual chemistry between them, but hadn't acted on it, though they'd been dating a month. Tonight was looking like a magic night, Christine had hoped, had thought, had felt earlier that day.

She was also stylish and attractive, her hair was long and smooth, and naturally wavy. Men sometimes likened it to the sea. She was intelligent, modest around the people she liked. Most of the time she had a great attitude; confident, fun and open-hearted.

The weakness she had, that she would happily tell others, was that she was quite sensitive. She saw it more as a strength but accepted that many others may not.

Serial Killers

She was honest and social, exactly the type of woman your average man wanted to bring home to meet his parents.

Christine was twenty-one years old, fit but not especially athletic, and she wondered if a gentle-natured, slim and sensitive lady like herself would be able to escape from – or heaven forbid – *defend* herself – from some knife-wielding maniac… who by the sound of things… kind of *enjoyed* stabbing young women like her to death. Her imagination wandered a little too far, and she thought… of a door being opened… a dark silent figure, a broad-shouldered powerful man, driven and possibly insane… raking a large butcher's knife across a sleeping beauty…

Her stomach shuddered, and she turned, in an instant she was too hot, the car seat was too unnatural in shape, the machinery of the vehicle was too awkward, too alien… a jolt of claustrophobia made its way through her body, but slow like a slug.

Patrick's fingernails caressed her leg nearest to him.

“Mmm… honey your hair’s so beautiful” he said, other hand pooling a lock of her brown mane, and Christine relaxed a little. She pushed the button to release the window a little, and the perfect amount of cool air came into the car. The song playing on the radio was one of her favourites, and she leaned the chair back a little.

The outside of his fingers caressed her mouth, so soft. He looked strong, but he was gentle. There were almost a million people in the city. Surely she was safe with him.

They kissed for a few minutes.

Christine liked Patrick’s golden hair, his strong squared-off face and his lively blue eyes. He had a strong face she told her friends, strong like his arms and chest, and Christine was a little excited to see him without so much clothing, without a big heavy jacket and a woolly hat. She stroked his shoulders, moving her fingertips around the muscle and bone, finger traipsing past the border of his T-shirt, flicking another button of his standard – but still classy – white office shirt.

He was also quite tall, which she liked.

The car was parked at the top a hill, on a scenic lookout. Patrick had picked her up about half an hour before they arrived at sunset, had a quick walk around, and got back in the car once it started getting dark on account of the cold.

There was nobody else near. Christine had not heeded the warnings from authorities to stay indoors around trusted loved ones. Until tonight, in Patrick's car alone with just him, the killings had felt far away.

They kissed and listened to music a little, until the DJ interrupted the music again, very excited and serious. She pulled away from kissing him as they both listened, but he still leaned in close to her.

"This just in: Police have made an official announcement. Late this afternoon two women have run away from a man police suspect as being a killer in eight murders. Both women gave independent descriptions, from the same area.

The suspect is a young male, probably in his late twenties, with minimal facial hair, just over six metres tall, broad-shouldered, slim and strong.

He had golden hair in a centre parting, a squarish face, and blue eyes. He was wearing leather shoes with two shades of beige, and light tan trousers and a white office shirt."

"Wow" said Patrick and Christine together.

"Police can also now confirm suspicions that today the body of another murdered lady was found. The killer used a large hunting knife like before. Police are almost certain this is the eighth victim of the killer. Police urge everyone to be careful, especially if they're alone. That description again, the killer is a young male probably in his late twenties, tall, broad-shouldered, with light golden hair quite short in a centre parting, a squarish face with minimal facial hair, and blue eyes. And again, that clothing was leather shoes that had two shades of beige, light tan trousers and a white office shirt. He was not wearing a tie at the time of the attempted attacks."

A jolt of mental lightning erupted in Christine's brain.

She wanted to scream.

Patrick was exactly as the announcer on the radio had described… he was wearing beige, or tan-coloured trousers.

The announcer reminded them of the numbers to call or text if they had any information specific to this case, and Patrick murmured he'd keep Christine safe, but she couldn't help writhing a little inside, as if her stomach was being peeled away from the rest of her and diving downwards into oblivion.

Her skin prickled as if it was enveloped in a sluggish trance, and Patrick's decisive, muscular bicep pressed against the back of her neck.

Christine felt like she was about to be eaten.

Her eyes forced themselves shut with fear, like little fists.

His shoes were leather, and two shades of beige.

His shirt was white.

Boring and nondescript thought Christine. Like what an office worker would wear. *Or a serial killer* disguised *as an office worker.*

He was broad-shouldered and in his late twenties. He barely had any facial hair. His short golden hair was in a centre parting.

Christine's hand reached wild, fumbling for the handle to open the passenger door. She pulled, useless as Patrick's lips, no longer sensual and sexy, but weird and dead and rubbery like a freak's, like a starving nocturnal animal's, pushed against her forehead, her nose, her own mouth.

"Mmm, babe, you're so cute Christine…" he murmured.

She wanted to talk, her mind reeling with the need to make a coherent sentence, to politely excuse herself – but she *wanted to RUN* – away from him! After all… surely he was about to murder her in cold blood, any second now!

She had to escape!

She forced her eyes open, but it was a Sisyphean struggle. She wanted to curl up on the floor of the car and cry in the fetal position.

“Babe… don’t worry, I’ll keep you safe” he urged in a whisper, eyes peering through hers, she wondered how far into her mind. She screamed inwardly, spiraling in terror at the idea of him following her, getting to know her, stalking her social media, befriending her mother her friends and family… *while plotting to kill her!*

“I think I really need to go” she heard a childish, meek voice peep up while her cavorting hand splayed all over the door, moving everywhere, except for the handle that opened it. *Where was it?* The mouth uttering her words was wobbling and craven with fight or flight, the hairs on her skin raised and tingling like little pylons.

“I need to visit muh-muh-muh-“

“Babe, no worries, I’m here, you’re safe with me-“

“I – I – need – to go see my muh- my mum, OK-”

His hands gripped her, a little tighter than before.

“Christine, what’s *wrong*, babe?”

Then it dawned on him.

“Oh, look, my clothes, right” he said, nodding, arms gesturing down his body, and she was so relieved his hands were off her she almost cried in happiness.

“Babe, there are *a million* outfits like this… that’s no doubt why this crazy guy is dressed like that, cos every guy in the city – or most of ‘em – have this in their wardrobe…. You remember that spring sale last year? *All* the clothing shops at the malls were rockin’ this look.”

Christine had found the handle, and was pulling and pulling and nothing was happening, but Patrick was still explaining.

“There were huge billboards, man, that shit was everywhere. It’s just, like, cheap Asian clothes, you know, but they look nice, so they sold a shitload.”

Christine could see the erection in his trousers as his arms moved around while he talked.

Her hand remembered the lock, and she pulled it upward, bumping her knuckles against the cold, blunt window.

“I’m worried about my mum” she said, less flaky than before, but not by much. “I – I – I wuh - wanna muh - make sure she’s safe, OK? So I have to go.”

She tilted towards him as she summoned the physical strength to open the car door, push it open and jump out – it felt, in her mind, like she had to fight a dragon – she didn’t want to have to move closer to him, but because of how she was sitting it seemed like the only way and her body did it before her mind could stop it.

But he grabbed her.

A hand on her knee, which moved up her inner thigh toward her groin. The other attached to the arm around her neck, keeping her close, absorbing the energy she needed to push herself away as the car door opened and a gush of cool night air came into the vehicle.

“Mmmm, babe, you’re so hot, babe, don’t worry about anything” he groaned, sliding her hand over his stomach. She was glad his hand was off her groin, but she shook with fear, he was trying to get her hand to slide under his T-shirt.

She screamed, finally. Not long, but with a little volume, and he laughed – not at her, not in a mean way, but just, it appeared, out of surprise. He regained his composure instantly.

“Fuck babe, what the hell is your problem? Do you know how many girls I turn away? I’m a fucking catch! I’m not a killer, everyone is dressed like this, don’t worry about it.”

His long arm reached over, pulling the door closed.

"You're letting all the hot air out babe, come on, let's get it steamy in here… and look, I know heaps of guys are crap in bed, but I… I rock, babe… I'll make you feel *reeeaaal* good, Christine…"

… His hand again on her thigh, moving in circles…

… She was whimpering and pushing him away…

… More kisses around her chin… her neck… as his weight pushed over her, chest pressing downward… one hand holding her head, as his spare hand pushed the lever that made the passenger seat lean back…

And Christine was more precarious than she had ever been, neck easily attainable to him. The fear boiled like lava in her head, her already-gentle arms felt pathetic and weak like little malnourished baby chicken wings, the floor of the car was at too obtuse an angle for her to push her feet against and bring her legs and weight to bear on escaping…

"Puh – Patrick! Please stop!"

The volume on the romantic music went up, then his hand began a gentle meandering up her thigh – then suddenly it was at her crotch, the zipper on her jeans down in a heartbeat.

“Come on babe, let’s get it on, let’s fuck already.”

His hand disappeared.

“I been looking forward to this for *ages…*”

Christine screamed again. The eighth victim had been so mutilated nobody could recognize her – or the police were being nice, and knew nobody wanted to see the hacked-up shards of their loved ones face – so they had identified her using other evidence. Christine almost vomited, her stomach lining tumbled about.

She knew what was going to happen – in a moment all manner of sick pieces fell into place:

– Patrick was the killer and he had a big jagged hunting knife under the seat!

Serial Killers

– He was going to kill her with it!

– He was going to ram it into her throat and her chest and stab her to death with it!

– He had stolen the car and it wasn't in his name so it couldn't be traced back to him!

– He would set fire to the car afterwards to remove any DNA or evidence of his presence!

– He probably had the super-flammable chemicals in the boot of the car already!

– He would leave town as soon as he'd killed her!

– Or he might go on killing more and more women!

– He knew her family and he would kill them too!

– He had arranged an alibi to prove he wasn't with her that night!

But in that storm of paranoia, a memory, a sound of clarity rung out like a bell.

Christine had a small pocket knife attached to her key ring. Her mother had given it to her when she turned eighteen, saying “dear I want you to have this, and don’t ever use it unless you really need to.”

It was only a small knife. The blade was only an inch long.

That had been a few years ago. Christine, for the most part, had hardly thought about the knife. Her hand leapt to the outside of her pocket, to make sure it was there.

Yes.

She dived into her pocket, silent and still as Patrick breathed on her.

One exhalation took forever.

He was reaching for the knife; the huge hunting knife he'd used to kill eight women with – and had tried to kill two more with – *and Christine was going to be number nine!* She was sure her bladder let go, and a jet of urine warmed her hips.

Her keys came up in her hand, and she slipped a thumbnail – thank God she had her nails at a practical length – into the blade's indentation and pulled. Her hand was shaky but good enough.

She pushed the blade upward into his throat, and a rain of blood began.

Christine was crying – rakish, awful sobs, as she stabbed him again and again, her arm jetting up and down in the space between the seats, and Patrick for a second, was shouting something – it may have been *"babe, what the hell?"* – or it may have been something completely different, but it didn't matter, because instead of words coming out of his mouth, wordy-sounding gusts of air bubbled out of his throat like swamp muck.

After the longest few seconds of Christine's life, she realized she was not only stabbing him, she was excavating the front of his neck, and screaming, gargling on the blood that fell into her mouth. Flecks of blood sprayed about her face and onto her eyelids, into her mouth, she had to scream, she couldn't not scream because killing him was so awful, while rivers of his blood spurted out of his neck and collar and face like hideous orgasms. He tried grabbing her, fighting back a little. There was so much blood in his body and it kept coming and it was sticky and pieces of his flesh fell on her, then at some point his arms gave up, his muscles stopped working, and he collapsed on her like a slab of meat, spasming a little, which pushed more blood out of him onto her and she screamed louder turning her head this way and that to avoid it but it felt so disgusting when it went all around her neck and slowly down her back and through her clothes that became clammy with it from the cold.

He rolled back, and she kept stabbing. Her arm was agony, exhausted. Soon, she was just pushing him with the knife. He went stiff, and limp. He must have weighed about one-and-a-half times what she did. Her bicep was molten with intensity, hand petrified and sticky.

Serial Killers

She lay there, crying.

He was dead.

Her shoulder flared hot with pain. She had to will her quivering hand to relax, and the keyring dropped onto the car floor, somewhere, anywhere. It didn't matter.

She wept a little, and a lot, sobs, trauma, mortality surging out of her, while the love songs kept playing on the radio.

She was forced to stop crying and forced to push him off her as it was too disgusting and uncomfortable. She wriggled sideways in the seat, and her other hand tried to feel out a good grip on him to push him off. Her eyes were firmly closed.

Matted hair was in her palm, but it was clotted and grotesque, and she whimpered. It brought on a new stagger of sobs, and she took his head from behind and pulled towards her feet, hoping she could at least bring the seat upright. A creaking, gurgling noise of sinew and groaning, the finality of air escaping lung punctured her ears.

It was a sound she'd never heard, had never thought would exist, and would hear in her nightmares for the rest of her life, and she wailed to no-one in pain. A squash of blood and flesh-muck, dregs of skin, lazily trailed out of the gigantic sinkhole in what was left of his throat, onto her thighs.

She shouted – angry – about how gross it all was (and remembered as a young girl always saying *"ooo, boys are gross"* with her friends) and found strength enough to push him, to reach and pull the lever to bring the seat up and lean forwards enough to allow it to move… for one awful second it felt like she was too heavy to let the seat up, that there was too much weight.

But Patrick collapsed, half on the passenger side, legs still on the driver's side. Blood continued to trickle out of him, and Christine moved her leg a little as some slid down to her ankle.

She was blinking a lot, it was awful but she took a tissue from the glove box and wiped her eyes. She sighed, enormous jagged breaths of relief, still crying.

She was safe, and the tendrils of a feeling of relief, of justification could almost be felt. But this was quickly forgotten when she saw pieces – chunks, lumps of his face and neck, half an ear – on the dashboard. She wished she hadn't looked down to see his graveyard of a face, the remnants of a handsome man – hell, even serial killers had mums and dads – and a fresh bout of hysterical screaming erupted from her as she began wondering how to explain it and what to say to Patrick's family… the tears washed away the blood a little, and she grabbed some more tissues… she blew her nose, and blinked… most of an eyeball sat on her groin, as if he was still interested in her vagina even after dying, as if he was still checking her out like some frat boy. She vomited, leaning forward, vomiting onto his corpse. She couldn't help it.

The love songs had changed; they'd relaxed a little. The frenzy that had erupted from her gentle nature was the stuff of mind-over-matter documentaries. Her arm had gone into some kind of automatic mode, a wild, super-conscious unconsciousness.

When she'd finished emptily retching, Christine wiped her face, blew her nose again, and opened the car door. The night air was cool, but not cold.

She cried some more, putting off the inevitable call to the police she'd have to make. She'd make it later. Surely, they'd understand if she didn't call them straight away. She'd never wanted to kill someone, she'd never cared for hiding bodies or torching evidence, honesty was the best policy in her mind. Surely, they'd let her off, they'd understand, because he had been about to cut her up with a huge hunting knife, he'd been reaching for it –

She wanted to see it. She looked back into the car, over his top half, toward his legs. He must have stashed the knife under the driver's seat, then he'd been reaching for it just before she killed him. She couldn't see any big hunting knife, meaning it would still be under the seat. She leaned over a little, holding her breath, to check. She stepped out of the car, walked around to the driver's side, and opened the door. She knelt down to look under the seat.

Nothing was there. But she did notice something else, by his foot.

It was a condom, mostly in its packet.

Dumbfounded, and with a heartbeat gaining intensity, Christine sat in the driver's seat.

The love song was interrupted by the same radio announcer as before, very excited.

"Everybody, police are very pleased to announce that they have caught the criminal that has killed eight people!"

Christine's stomach churned as she tried to avoid looking at Patrick's body.

"His name is Jeffrey Platt, twenty-seven years old, and he was caught this evening after locals reported him suspiciously moving through the back yard of a lady living alone. He had a large knife with him and has now confessed to the other murders. DNA and other evidence at previous scenes have corroborated this."

The announcer remarked that this was wonderful news in what had been a harrowing time for everyone in the city. The announcer expressed deepest condolences to victims' families and gave a few suggestions on where people could turn to for help – social workers, various community and charity groups.

Christine groaned. Patrick had not been the killer at all. He had been sleazy, creepy, a bit cocky and egotistic… but not a killer. Christine looked around again for a hunting knife, but there wasn't one.

Drenched in blood and dumbfounded, Christine began crying again as the distant sound of birds chirping and insects mating could be heard in the still night air, mingling with the love song playing over the car radio. They all seemed to become louder and jarring and louder, antagonistic. After a few minutes, Christine didn't know if she was crying or laughing or screaming or hyperventilating or going mad or about to start stabbing her own throat just to end the shock of it all, or just *what* the hell was going on.

Follow Arthur and his work here:

PIGGY

BY

COLIN C. MARTIN

"I'm sorry. The officer is currently involved in a case and hasn't had time to come and request the CCTV footage." Ian looked at the PCSO with a mixture of bewilderment and disgust. This stringy, thin, little excuse of a man was what was on the streets these days. They were employed to help with anti-social behaviour, dissuade young people from getting involved in gang activity. A supposed helping hand to the police while they focussed on serious crime.

Ian hadn't really had many dealings with them until he started his current role a year previously. He'd worked in retail before on several occasions. Usually as a stop gap while he was waiting on another contract to come through. He wasn't fussy when it came to do what was needed to pay the bills. A job was a job at the end of the day.

Never in his life though had he dealt with this level of antagonism than he was right now. Even during his stint on the door in some of the roughest night clubs in town during his early 20's was nothing compared to this constant aggro. Then again, things were dealt with differently back then.

The little shits were practically begging you to do something. Squaring up to your face, their friends with camera phones at the ready to try and get that viral clip so that they could play the victim. Ian knew the game that was being played. Cowardly filth that had a chip on their shoulder and something to prove always behaved in the same way. *It has never changed and never will* He thought to himself. However, until now there had always been a way to push back or at least get something resolved about these types of situations.

What Ian wasn't prepared for was the total intransigence and borderline complicity of the authorities. Despite having windows and furniture broken, as well as customers and staff getting harassed daily, they simply refused to help. He considered himself a reasonably diligent manager, ensuring each incident was logged on the company's reporting system. This not only created a record for the current campaign of harassment his shop was experiencing but also provided a mechanism for the police to gather the CCTV footage to then identify the ringleaders and take the appropriate action.

Yet, for some reason the Police and PCSO's simply refused to take the next step. Even after three months of escalating harassment and a colleague having her hand broken, they wouldn't even make the CCTV request. A formal request had to be submitted via email or served as a court order to comply with data protection law. Ian found himself perplexed by this mentality. Maybe if he'd been brought up in a soft middle class home like the university gap year students that decided to put on a uniform and cosplay at being a Police Officer/Social Worker he could maybe understand the thinking. Ian was simply on the wrong tier. Justice wasn't meant for him it seemed.

Ian scoffed at his naivety. He'd read the news reports about lawless Britian and how the country was being held hostage by gangs of criminal youths. These creatures were dragged up as opposed to being raised by their parents. Most of whom either spent most of their time doped out of their heads, in the local pub or in jail. There was something detached about seeing these incidents on camera phone, CCTV and news footage. From the safety of a screen, it was one thing. It was something else entirely living with it day to day.

What the videos and reels didn't show you was the tension that filled the air once 15:30 came and the schools came out. Kids so cock sure of themselves that causing a ruckus in their uniforms didn't bother them. Then of course there was 16:00 when the older kids got out. Ian referred to them as the 'professionals' These were the career criminals in waiting. Testing out their skills and asserting their street authority, ready to sign up with the local gangsters once they had proved their worth. What the reels also didn't show was the ratty little faces of the malnourished little cunts who tried to square up to you. The type that you could simply shake like a rag doll and end them without even having to throw a punch. All the kids looked like this, dressed in their dingy tracksuits with their shitty looking slides trying to give it big licks. It was the uniform of the belligerent. Piggy didn't look like this though. That's what made him stand out.

Piggy was head and shoulders taller the rest. He was a slightly older teenager, still young in relative terms. He was filled out a lot more than his peers. He'd obviously stolen more than his fair share of lunch money in the playground and had kids bringing him snacks when they raided the sandwich shop on the high street. Despite this also being a daily occurrence nobody seemed to get arrested. The police knew who Piggy was.

Piggy had a name apparently, Ian had heard one of the PCSO's mention it. They knew Piggy was the ringleader, yet Piggy was never touched. This was Piggy's territory. His playground.

Piggy hadn't liked it when Ian threw him out of the shop and banned him and his friends from returning. Ian remembered the first couple of encounters with Piggy and co when he first took on the role. Piggy and friends would come in and make a point of lounging on one of the sofas. If not provided with enough attention, then they would start jumping on the sofa's beds and other furniture. Sure enough things would soon get thrown and broken before they would leave just before the police arrived.

It only took Ian a week to figure out the pattern of behaviour and begin counter measures. He always believed in the principle of prevention was better than a cure and by simply making sure that he was close to the doors when the little shits arrived, he was able to prevent them from entry. That's when everything kicked off.

It appeared that Piggy didn't like being told what to do, or having his fun spoiled. It started with kids on stolen Lime bikes racing into the store to crash into things before running off. Bottles of fizzy drink would be shaken and thrown in to explode everywhere. Head office wouldn't help of course. They could only justify the cost of a security guard on the weekends, not that they were any use of course. Most of them hid out the back of the store on their phones and were constantly taking breaks for one thing or another. Ian was getting to the end of his tether.

Ian remembered the day that he snapped. He had primed himself for weeks waiting for the explosion. Just that one look, one snarky comment or shove. He knew the minute that he lashed out he was going to prison. Assaulting a minor had serious consequences these days. Even a slap to the head was going to land him at least two to three years. Random bursts of anger woke him up in the middle of the night, ruining his sleep. This had been a constant for a month now. He was tired, run down and weary. All it took was a milkshake.

Serial Killers

"Look. I have the list collated with our company references and the dates and times of the incidents since May." Ian was speaking to Holly, the team leader of the PCSOs. Holly was 4"2 and could barely fit into her uniform. Ian had seen Army Cadets better turned out than her. She would have been worth pity if it wasn't for her stuck up, snarky tone as if his complaints were a bother and she had so many better things to do. Ian despised her and had no doubt that she saw him as something to be scraped off her shoe. "Look sir! We appreciate you giving us this. We are looking into things. It just takes time to go through the process."

"Process? This has been going on for three solid months now. All I want you to do is…" SPLASH! The cup smacked against the side of Ian's head, spilling the contents over his face and shirt. This was the moment he had been waiting for. He had been expecting it for a while now. What he didn't expect was the calm detachment that came over him instead of the explosive anger he was anticipating. Even the shouts of "Fuck you, Ginger!" as the kids sped off sounded like they were underwater or very far away.

"Oh, my goodness! Are you alright?"

Even when she was trying to show concern, Holly had a snarky undertone to it. *She is probably just annoyed that it didn't happen to her so that she could go off sick with PTSD*. Ian thought.

It was a banana milkshake. Ian hated banana. He was going to have the stench of this up his nostrils for the next couple of days. It was that moment that Ian realised that he'd had enough. He could quit this job and spend his time again commuting into the city or get another job in another shitty little town with its own group of Chavs.

There was nowhere to go. Everything was getting worse. Ian could feel it. Even though he tried to avoid the news, the parts that got through was nothing but doom and gloom. Society was falling apart. Now that he'd experienced the full brunt of it, he was filled with despair. He may as well just end himself now and be done with it. Then Ian saw the image of Piggy smirking in his mind. His despondency quickly turned to rage, followed by a cold, cold anger. No, there was another way.

Ian had never stalked anyone before, never mind a gang of kids. He was going to have to take his time with this. Rushing in would only get him caught or cornered by the gang itself and possibly stabbed. This was London after all, the city of shit! Finding the kids was easy. Ian was amused that the extent of their lives revolved around the total of six streets, including the tenement block where they lived. *Didn't anyone remember why these things were torn down in the 90s?* Ian thought. Maybe he was old enough to remember the crime ridden cesspits that scoured the landscape in his youth. Havens for crime and depravation. Symbols of hopelessness and lost causes. It seemed stupid when the councils started building them again. *It's funny how the historical cycle keeps repeating*. Ian thought as he watched the gang in their natural habitat.

They had taken over the local park, effectively making it a no-go area for the other residents. Ian could feel the tension in the air as he passed by each night. He had picked up a bunch of cheap tracksuits from a Sports Direct in the next town. He decided not to constantly wear dark clothing, lest he draw the attention of the gang or the local authorities on the rare occasion that they decided to patrol.

The police hid in their cruisers and very rarely ventured out, instead relying on CCTV to capture incidents. Most of the cameras were broken or vandalised in this area. This suited Ian just fine.

Ian had been stalking the area for over a week now. He still wasn't sure what he was going to do. The reconnaissance aspect hadn't been that difficult. Ian quickly ascertained that the gang members were brain dead morons who moped around, caused trouble then slunk away back to their flats when they started to get tired. The problem, Ian realised was that they left in groups. There was no easy way to single one or even two out. Ian thought that this was probably a subconscious action, borne out of their lifestyle. Like a herd of buffalo roaming the plains as a mass for safety. Ian was starting to get frustrated, thinking that he was never going to figure out a solution, then it happened.

"I'll fucking cut you bruv!"

One of the bigger kids smashed a bottle and started waving it around. Something was obviously done or said that broke the Chav code. Maybe it was the fact that the gang hadn't found anyone to harass that evening and needed to vent off some energy.

Either way, an opportunity was presenting itself. Ian moved back into the shadows to watch the proceedings.

“Easy bruv. I meant no disrespect. I was only talking to her, like. I know she’s your girl.”

Ian recognised the smaller kid as ‘Max’. One of the dipshits that had spat at him through the shop door one occasion. Max was one of the scrawny, but taller kids in the group. He was almost as big of a mouthpiece as Piggy. Maybe nature would take care of itself, and Ian wouldn’t have to waste his time on this nonsense anymore. Some hope!

“Go on then, fuck off!”

The words of the older kid were slurred slightly. More than likely because of drugs or alcohol. The gang had ready access to these things. Despite his bravado, Max knew that he was beat.

“Fine! Fuck you bruv. I wasn’t doin nothin!”

Max stormed off away from the playground area. None of the other kids tried to go with him or try to calm things down. That's just the way it was with their lifestyle.

Ian started walking away towards the back of the flats and circled around. He knew that to follow directly would bring the attention of the rest of the gang and ruin his plans. He had spent too long on this to mess up now. As he walked quickly along the parallel row of buildings, he put the Stanley knife that he had brought with him back in his pocket. The gang leader had given him an idea.

"Fucking cunt! I never touched his girl. She's a fucking skank anyway!"

Max was mumbling to himself as he walked home. He'd been humiliated in front of the gang, and it was agitating him. He didn't like to feel small. He wasn't that smart and was always behind in school. His mother was always out on the piss down at the slapper's flat at the end of the row and he'd never met his dad. His mum probably never even knew who he was.

He was angry and wanted to lash out. Max guessed he could go and annoy the ginger manager at the furniture store tomorrow after school. That always gave him a laugh.

Max saw stars as the punch landed on the side of his neck. He immediately dropped to the ground dazed. Ian stood over him surprised at how quickly the little shit had gone down. Maybe he should have pulled his punch a little, but he needed this to be done quickly. Time was of the essence in these neighbourhoods. You never knew who was going to walk by. Ian immediately set to work stabbing the boy in the neck. He had picked up a broken bottle on the way to intercept Max. There was no shortage of them lying around. Another sign of the run-down area they were in. Max barely had time to register what was happening to him as the jagged edge of the bottle ripped into his neck. Blood spurted everywhere as Ian stabbed in a frenzy. Within mere seconds the lights went out in Max's eyes and his body went limp. Ian stood over him panting.

Adrenaline was coursing through Ian, and he was having trouble processing everything. In the blink of an eye he had went from an ordinary citizen to a stone-cold killer. It took less than ten seconds to carry out the deed.

He looked down at the boy who stared upwards with lifeless eyes. Blood was still spurting from his neck and pooling around him. In the blink of an eye one of Ian's tormentors was gone.

The rational side of Ian's mind kicked in. He didn't have time to revel or process. He needed to get away. He started to quickly walk away. Part of his brain was screaming at him to run, but he held it in check. That would only attract attention. Ian waited until he was at least a block away before dropping the bottle into a litter bin. He stripped off the latex gloves he was wearing and stuffed them into the pouch pocket of his hoodie.

Ian made his way to an alley behind a take-away restaurant he had marked out during his trips. It was dark with no CCTV. He stopped to take off the oversize hoodie he was wearing stuffed it into the backpack he wore underneath. He turned it inside out in case there was any blood.

He quickly grabbed a wet wipe and cleaned his face. Ian wasn't sure if he had been splashed, but this was part of the plan. Taking a moment to catch his breath and slow his heart rate down, Ian then walked slowly and deliberately onto the main street.

He casually crossed the street and away from the estate where the gang hung out. He had parked his e-bike a little out of the way so that it wouldn't be noticed or stolen. It was a purchase he had made recently for the purpose of his mission. It was much less noticeable than taking public transportation or driving his car into town. CCTV and ULEZ cameras tracked everything these days. Although not a perfect solution, the e-bike allowed him to make a quick getaway without getting noticed. Nobody knew that he had the bike, and he didn't ride it around during the day so that his profile wouldn't become recognisable. Ian made his way home.

Things were quiet for a couple of days. The death of Max apparently had an impact. By the end of the week news had gotten out that one of the kids had been killed in a gang dispute. Another victim of London's knife crime epidemic. Ian had to resist the urge to correct customers that it was a bottle, not a knife when they recounted the story.

Ian thought that he would have at least felt a little bit of remorse or guilt for his actions. Maybe it was the instant calm that seemed to fall over the area after the incident. The kids seemed to scuttle straight home after school and not even hang around in the High Street. For once since he'd started in this job, Ian knew peace. *Is that all it took?* He thought. One stabbing and they would see sense and change their ways. Part of him naively hoped that it would be the case. He enjoyed getting on with his day-to-day activities. Routine agreed with him. Like most people he just wanted to earn a living and get on with his life. It wasn't going to last, however. This was London after all.

The beep, beep, beep of the stolen Lime bikes signalled the return of the scrotes in force. Three or four days of peace had obviously been too much for them and it was time to cause havoc again.

The coffee table splintered like matchwood when two of the kids jumped onto it. Their shrieks of joy drowning out the cracking sound of the wood. Piggy, of course was standing in the doorway egging them on.

“How ya doin ginger? Havin a nice day?” He crooned.

Ian sighed inwardly and picked up the phone.

“999, what service do you require?”

“I need the police please.”

Once again, he went through the rigmarole of giving his details and describing the incident, explaining that it was currently ongoing and the gang was still in the store. Ian could have sworn that the emergency services were hiring former GP receptionists for the role these days. Their questioning tone seemed to imply that his call was a major hassle, and he really shouldn’t be bothering them.

“I’m sorry sir, units aren’t going to be able to attend for at least forty minutes.” The operator droned.

Ian got the CAD reference and jotted it down. The kids had decided to move on at this point, as they usually did once he started providing detailed descriptions. It wasn't like they covered their faces or hid from the CCTV cameras. Everything at this point felt like going through the motions. A pointless exercise in a pointless as part of a pointless society. Ian decided at that moment his actions weren't going to be pointless anymore.

He had spent his evenings scoping out areas that he could enact his plan. The urban sprawl of London provided little in the way of privacy or space. Like an all-consuming beast it had swallowed up the surrounding towns and hamlets. Like a cancer spreading it withered fields and open spaces to scar with the lesions and boils that were the HMO's and social housing blocks. The pus that burst from them were the anti-social delinquents that Ian now hunted.

One thing that remained surprisingly constant were the riverside areas. The industrial areas of the boatyards and dry docks seemed relatively untouched. The husks of abandoned narrow boats lay around like corpses waiting for the vultures to come and pick at them.

In the evenings most of the areas had little to no activity. The poorer areas seemed to have the most going on, probably some illegal or nefarious activity. Ian thought it best to stay away from these yards. Eventually after a week of searching he found the perfect place. Quiet with several work sheds. These units also had running water and electricity. This would be ideal for what he had planned, Ian thought grimly.

Getting Piggy and at least some of his friends there was going to be the real challenge. Obviously, the e-bike wasn't going to do the job. Ian felt a sense of frustration as he set out his equipment in the work shed he had commandeered. It wasn't in use, he'd checked, and he didn't want to rent anywhere, lest someone was able to identify him after the fact. There was every chance that he was going to get caught after what he had planned. However, it made no sense to plan for failure. Ian planned to make a statement and whether his name was going to be linked to it, or not. The statement was going to be made.

"Mum?"

Ben called out as he entered their flat. He wasn't expecting her to be there but called out anyway. It was the weekend, and she'd more than likely be down at Sharon's. They always gathered there for a couple of bottles of While Lightning and a few joints. Ben didn't mind; he was used to it. He'd grab some noodles and head to bed. He'd had a couple of drinks himself, and Jenny had given him a nosh earlier. He was feeling good.

Despite his size, Ben had little strength when it came to struggling against the rag was being pressed to his face. Someone had crept up on him from behind. He barely had time to register the speed and ferocity of the attack as he crumpled to the floor losing consciousness.

Ben started to come to slowly. His head was throbbing. The scent and sensation of whatever it was that he breathed in still lingered in his nostrils. When he tried to swallow that's when he realised that something was in his mouth. His brain was foggy, and he couldn't work out what it was. All he knew was that it was tight, uncomfortable and he couldn't close his mouth properly.

When he started to wretch, that's when he realised that his head was facing downwards. He started to panic and stand up that's when he understood that he was tied up, unable to move.

"Ahhh! You're awake Piggy. That's good. I'm nearly ready for you. I'm just finishing up with a couple of your friends."

Ben knew that voice instantly. Even in his muddled state he recognised the ginger cunt at the furniture shop. He didn't have any problems on the High Street until that fucker arrived. Now the police were constantly annoying him as well as the community cops. When he got out of this, he was going to fuck him up.

The sound of a barrel scraping along the floor jarred him from his thoughts. This was followed by the sound of a lid popping then a series of thumps as items were thrown into it.

"Nggg, Hmmm Arggg"

Ben tried to shout some obscenities but whatever was in his mouth prevented him from doing so.

“Oh, sorry about the belt. It was the best thing I could think of that would keep you quiet and stop you from choking. Even though this place is isolated. We can’t run the risk of getting disturbed, can we?”

Ben heard footsteps as the store manager walked towards him. The reality of the situation was starting to dawn on him. He started to struggle frantically.

“Now, now Piggy. There’s no point getting yourself upset. There will be plenty of opportunity for that in a few moments.”

Ian patted the boy on the head in an almost fatherly manner. It had taken a while to set this up, but he could see now that it was time well spent. The workbench was the heavy, iron type, used for working on propellers and other parts of a boat. He had picked up steel cabling and steel plumbers clips, which he had used to secure the boy. Ian was quite proud of himself when he had thought of the idea of securing each of the boys’ fingers to the legs of the bench using the clips. Steel wouldn’t fray or snap like rope or cord would and would also conduct heat and electricity.

Ian still couldn't believe how swiftly the night's activities had gone. He had needed two of the other kids to send his message, they didn't have to be alive though when he brought them to this place. Chavs seemed to get more amorous at the weekend he'd noticed. It seemed to be something that was bred into them. Copulate, breed, multiply and spread their misery. It was a simple matter of tracking down two who had sloped off to shag each other in an alley. An iron bar took care of them quickly. Ian wasn't even sure if it registered with them when he caved their skulls in as they groped and kissed each other. It was a simple matter of loading them up into the van he had brought from the yard. The tarp and single mattress he had also brought with him helped to soak up any leaks. He would burn that when he was finished.

Then it was just a matter of waiting for Piggy. I don't think he even realised that his mother was a prostitute. Off she went 9 o'clock on the dot to ply her trade. Most of her transactions were 'friendly' it appeared. She went to her friends' house where they both entertained their regulars. Sometimes for money, other times for drugs and booze. It's amazing what you could pick up if you just hung around, listening to the local fish wives gossiping. Most times she never locked her door when she left, this worked out for Ian just fine.

He finished loading up the happy couple into the barrel then went back to Piggy. He had planned out what he wanted to do but wasn't sure if he wanted to begin. When he had planned this Ian had envisioned days of inflicting torture and beatings on the three of the little shits. Breaking a bone for every taunt and a cut or a slice for every sleepless night that he had because of these bastards. He was also pragmatic. Ian knew that he was on limited time. Even in this rotten city three kids going missing would raise some eyebrows and even their drug addled parents would notice that they were gone.

Ian opened the jar of homemade smelling salts and wafted it under Piggy's nose. The boy scrunched his face then jolted awake. Panic appeared in his eyes and he became fully awake.

"There we go. Now I have your attention. I want to talk to you briefly. Tell me Piggy. Every time you came around and made my life hell, was it worth it?"

Serial Killers

Ben grunted and tried to shout out as he swivelled his head to face his captor. The angle in which his neck hung over the edge of the workbench made it difficult. Suddenly he yelped as a strong hand gripped him by the hair and forced his head vertically. A cold, hard pair of eyes stared into his.

“WELL, WAS IT?”

He could clearly see the face of the store manager who he used to taunt. Ben used to get off on the fact that he knew the guy wanted to punch him but couldn’t. Society’s rules made it easy. He was a minor. That gave him a free pass until he was eighteen. Yes, some of his mates had done a stint in the Young Offender’s Centre, but you had to be proper mental to end up there. He had learned how to play the game.

What he saw now though frightened him. This was someone who didn’t want to play by the rules anymore. He reminded him of Oggy, the local drug dealer who also ran the gangs in the area. Oggy would stick a knife in you as soon as look at you. As long as you obeyed the rules and showed respect you were fine. With this guy, however. Ben realised that he wasn’t going to be fine.

Tears started to well up in his eyes as Ian looked at him impassively.

“It’s too late for tears now Piggy. It was too late for your mates as well. I let them go quickly though. You don’t get that consideration Piggy. I’m going to take a bit of time with you. I’m going to cut bits of you off, I’m going to stick things inside you. I’m going to burn you, then kill you Piggy.”

The cold delivery of the monologue shook Ben to his core. He could feel the intense hatred of each word and the cold detachment of someone who had snapped. Although he couldn’t articulate the words himself. He could feel the intent.

“Alright then Piggy. I think it’s time to begin.”

Ian let the boy’s head drop then reached for the shears.

Serial Killers

When Ian arrived for work on Monday morning, the area was cordoned off. One of the residents had left their flat in the morning to find a gruesome display in the playground. A flayed and burned body had been strung up over the climbing frame. The face, what was left of the face was contorted into an eyeless scream. The body had been impaled with a steel rod which had been used to stabilise the corpse and splay it out for all to see. The fingers, toes and genitals of the victim were missing.

As if that wasn't enough for the macabre display a multitude of body parts had been arranged around the perimeter of the climbing frame. The two heads placed at the feet of the upright body indicated multiple victims.

It took a week for forensics to identify the body as that of Ben Williams, thirteen years of age and known as a local troublemaker in the area. His companions were identified as Sarah Jennings, fourteen and Tyrone Williams, sixteen. They were also known to police as local gang members who took part in anti-social behaviour and carried out low-level crimes in the area.

It was another day before Ian could open the store again. All things considered he was grateful for the day off. He had been awake for close to forty-eight hours at that point without stopping. The chance to recuperate would be handy for when the police came.

It wasn't until the Wednesday that the investigating officer came around. Strangely enough, he had Holly, the lead PCSO with him. *Must be using this investigation to grease her way up the pole.* Ian thought.

"Good morning, I'm Detective Sergeant Billings." The officer said.

Ian shook his hand.

"How can I help you, Sergeant?" He asked.

"I am sure you aware of the incident that has taken place in the local community grounds." He said. "We are trying to get as much information as possible, even the tiniest piece could help us greatly with our enquiries."

The story of the brutal slayings had been all over the media at this point. Even for London, this had been considered brutal. Speculation had run rampant about rival gangs carrying out initiation rituals. Voodoo and Satanic cults in the area to cannibals roaming the streets. People were frightened and the kids stayed at home these days. In the back of Ian's mind, he wondered how many weeks' peace could be garnished from the incident.

"Of course, Sergeant, happy to help."

"Dan, please." The detective insisted.

"No problem, Dan. Sadly this area has been going to the dogs for a while. I'm sure that Holly has briefed you up." He nodded towards the PCSO who kept a straight face.

"Yes, one of the reasons why we are here is to gain access to your CCTV. We believe the local youths hung around here in particular. Maybe an interaction could give us insight as to who they were meeting or if another gang moved into the area. This runs twenty-fours a day. Is that correct?"

Ian nodded.

“Yes, we have multiple cameras throughout the store and at the front of the shop. Everything is held externally on the company’s servers. Of course, sharing it won’t be a problem. There is just one thing we will need.”

“Oh! What’s that?” The detective asked.

“You will have to submit a formal request for the footage in writing.”

Follow Colin and his work here:

Thank you for taking the time to enjoy these stories. Please be sure to follow our authors by using the QR codes and pick up their work. Until next time our friends. Remember to keep it creepy, keep it HORRORific!

Embark on a HORRORific journey with our anthology series
HORRORific Tales
Volume One
(Hauntings)
HORRORific Tales
Volume Two
(Cryptids)
HORRORific Tales
Volume Three
(Serial Killers)

Available Now!
Mistress of Darkness:
Stories of the Macabre
(Volume 1)
Del Gibson

Printed in Dunstable, United Kingdom

65724629R00198